J. M. COETZEE

J. M. Coetzee's work includes *Waiting for the Barbarians*, *Life & Times of Michael K*, *Boyhood*, *Youth*, *Disgrace*, *Summertime*, *The Childhood of Jesus*, *The Schooldays of Jesus* and *The Death of Jesus*. He is the first writer to have won the Booker Prize twice and was awarded the Nobel Prize in Literature in 2003.

ALSO BY J. M. COETZEE

Late Essays 2006–2017
Inner Workings: Literary Essays 2000–2005
Stranger Shores: Essays 1986–1999
The Childhood of Jesus
The Schooldays of Jesus
The Death of Jesus
Summertime
Youth
Boyhood
Slow Man
Elizabeth Costello
Age of Iron
Dusklands
Foe
In the Heart of the Country
Disgrace
Life & Times of Michael K
The Master of Petersburg
Waiting for the Barbarians
Three Stories
Diary of a Bad Year

J. M. COETZEE

The Pole

& Other Stories

VINTAGE

1 3 5 7 9 10 8 6 4 2

Vintage is part of the Penguin Random House group of companies
whose addresses can be found at global.penguinrandomhouse.com

First published in Vintage in 2024
First published in Great Britain by Harvill Secker in 2023
First published in Australia by The Text Publishing Company in 2023

Copyright © J. M. Coetzee 2023

J. M. Coetzee has asserted his right to be identified as the author of this
Work in accordance with the Copyright, Designs and Patents Act 1988

The title story, 'The Pole', was first published in Argentina under
the title *El Polaco*, by El Hilo de Adriana, Buenos Aires, 2022

Page design by W. H. Chong
Typeset by J&M Typesetting

penguin.co.uk/vintage

Printed and bound in Great Britain by Clays Ltd, Elcograf S.p.A.

The authorised representative in the EEA is Penguin Random House Ireland,
Morrison Chambers, 32 Nassau Street, Dublin D02 YH68

A CIP catalogue record for this book is available from the British Library

ISBN 9781529920635

Penguin Random House is committed to a sustainable future for
our business, our readers and our planet. This book is made from
Forest Stewardship Council® certified paper.

CONTENTS

THE POLE
1

AS A WOMAN GROWS OLDER
149

THE OLD WOMAN AND THE CATS
179

THE GLASS ABATTOIR
207

HOPE
233

THE DOG
243

ACKNOWLEDGMENTS
253

The Pole

& Other Stories

THE POLE

ONE

1. The woman is the first to give him trouble, followed soon afterwards by the man.

2. At the beginning he has a perfectly clear idea of who the woman is. She is tall and graceful; by conventional standards she may not qualify as a beauty but her features—dark hair and eyes, high cheekbones, full mouth—are striking and her voice, a low contralto, has a suave attractive power. Sexy? No, she is not sexy, and certainly not seductive. She might have been sexy when she was young—how can she not have been with a figure like that?—but now, in her forties, she goes in for a certain remoteness. She walks—one notices this particularly—without swinging her hips, gliding across the floor erect, even stately.

That is how he would sum up her exterior. As for her self, her soul, there is time for that to reveal itself. Of one thing he is convinced: she is a good person, kind, friendly.

3. The man is more troublesome. In concept, again, he is perfectly clear. He is a Pole, a man of seventy, a vigorous seventy, a concert pianist best known as an interpreter of Chopin, but a controversial interpreter: his Chopin is not at all Romantic but on the contrary somewhat austere, Chopin as inheritor of Bach. To that extent he is an oddity on the concert scene, odd enough to draw a small but discerning audience in Barcelona, the city to which he has been invited, the city where he will meet the graceful, soft-spoken woman.

But barely has the Pole emerged into the light than he begins to change. With his striking mane of silver hair, his idiosyncratic renderings of Chopin, the Pole promises to be a distinct enough personage. But in matters of soul, of feeling, he is troublingly opaque. At the piano he plays with soul, undeniably; but the soul that rules him is Chopin's, not his own. And if that soul strikes one as unusually dry and severe, it may point to a certain aridity in his own temperament.

4. Where do they come from, the tall Polish pianist and the elegant woman with the gliding walk, the banker's wife who occupies her days in good works? All year they have been knocking at the door, wanting to be let

in or else dismissed and laid to rest. Now, at last, has their time come?

5. The invitation to the Pole comes from a Circle that stages monthly recitals in the Sala Mompou, in Barcelona's Gothic Quarter, and has been doing so for decades. The recitals are open to the public, but tickets are expensive and the audience tends to be wealthy, aging, and conservative in its tastes.

The woman in question—her name is Beatriz—is a member of the board that administers the series. She performs this role as a civic duty, but also because she believes that music is good in itself, as love is good, or charity, or beauty, and good furthermore in that it makes people better people. Though well aware that her beliefs are naive, she holds to them anyway. She is an intelligent person but not reflective. A portion of her intelligence consists in an awareness that excess of reflection can paralyse the will.

6. The decision to invite the Pole, whose name has so many w's and z's in it that no one on the board even tries to pronounce it—they refer to him simply as 'the Pole'—is arrived at only after some soul-searching.

His candidacy was proposed not by her, Beatriz, but by her friend Margarita, the animating spirit behind the concert series, who in her youth studied at the conservatory in Madrid and knows much more about music than she does.

The Pole, says Margarita, led the way for a new generation of Chopin interpreters in his native land. She circulates a review of a concert he gave in London. According to the reviewer, the fashion for a hard, percussive Chopin—Chopin as Prokofiev—has had its day. It was never anything but a Modernist reaction against the branding of the Franco-Polish master as a delicate, dreamy, 'feminine' spirit. The emerging, historically authentic Chopin is soft-toned and Italianate. The Pole's revisionary reading of Chopin, even if somewhat over-intellectualized, is to be lauded.

She, Beatriz, is not sure that she wants to hear an evening's worth of historically authentic Chopin, nor, more pertinently, whether the rather staid Circle will take kindly to it. But Margarita feels strongly about the matter, and Margarita is her friend, so she gives her her support.

The invitation to the Pole accordingly went out, with a proposed date and a proposed fee, and was accepted. Now the day has arrived. He has flown in from Berlin, has been met at the airport and driven to his hotel. The plan for the evening is that, after the recital, she, together with Margarita and Margarita's husband, will take him out to dinner.

7. Why will Beatriz's own husband not be one of the party? The answer: because he never attends Concert Circle events.

8. The plan is simple enough. But then there is a hitch. On the morning in question Margarita telephones to say that she has fallen ill. That is the rather formal term she uses: *caído enferma*, fallen ill. What has she fallen ill with? She does not say. She is vague, deliberately so, it would seem. But she will not be coming to the recital. Nor will her husband. Therefore will she, Beatriz, please take over the duties of hospitality, that is to say, arrange to have their guest conveyed from hotel to auditorium in good time, and entertain him afterwards, if he wants to be entertained, so that when he returns to his native country he will be able to say to his friends, *Yes, I had a good time in Barcelona, on the whole. Yes, they took good care of me.*

'Very well,' says Beatriz, 'I will do it. And I hope you get better soon.'

9. She has known Margarita since they were children together at the nuns' school; she has always admired her friend's spirit, her enterprise, her social aplomb. Now she must take her place. What will it entail, entertaining a man on a fleeting visit to a strange city? Surely, at his age, he will not expect sex. But he will certainly expect to be flattered, even flirted with. Flirting is not an art she has ever cared to master. Margarita is different. Margarita has a light touch with men. She, Beatriz, has more than once, with amusement, watched her friend go about her conquests. But she has no wish to imitate her. If their guest has high expectations in the department of flattery, he is going to be disappointed.

10. The Pole is, according to Margarita, a 'truly memorable' pianist. She heard him in the flesh, in Paris. Is it possible that something happened between the two of them, Margarita and the Pole, in the flesh; and that, having engineered his visit to Barcelona, Margarita is at the last minute having cold feet? Or has her husband finally had enough, and issued a fiat? Is that how

'falling ill' is to be understood? Why must everything be so complicated!

And now she must take care of the stranger! There is no reason to expect he speaks Spanish. What if he does not speak English either? What if he is the kind of Pole who speaks French? The only regulars in the Concert Circle who speak French are the Lesinskis, Ester and Tomás; and Tomás, in his eighties, is becoming infirm. How will the Pole feel when, instead of the vivacious Margarita, he is offered the decrepit Lesinskis?

She is not looking forward to the evening. What a life, she thinks, the life of an itinerant entertainer! The airports, the hotels, all different yet all the same; the hosts to put up with, all different yet all the same: gushing middle-aged women with bored attendant husbands. Enough to quench whatever spark there is in the soul.

At least she does not gush. Nor does she chatter. If after his performance the Pole wants to retreat into moody silence, she will be moody right back.

11. Producing a concert, making sure that everything runs smoothly, is no small feat. The burden has now fallen squarely on her. She spends the afternoon at the

concert hall, chivvying the staff (their supervisor is, in her experience, dilatory), ticking off details. Is it necessary to list the details? No. But it is by her attention to detail that Beatriz will prove that she possesses the virtues of diligence and competence. By comparison, the Pole will show himself to be impractical, unenterprising. If one can conceive of virtue as a quantity, then the greater part of the Pole's virtue is spent on his music, leaving hardly any behind for his dealings with the world; whereas Beatriz's virtue is expended evenly in all directions.

12. Publicity photographs show a man with a craggy profile and a shock of white hair staring into the middle distance. The accompanying biography says that Witold Walczykiewicz was born in 1943 and made his concert debut at the age of fourteen. It lists prizes he has won and some of his recordings.

She wonders what it was like to be born in 1943, in Poland, in the middle of a war, with nothing to eat but cabbage-and-potato-peel soup. Is one's physical development stunted? And what of the spirit? Will Witold W prove to bear, in his bones, in his spirit, the marks of a starved childhood?

A baby wailing in the night, wailing with hunger.

She was born in 1967. In 1967 no one in Europe had to eat cabbage soup: no one in Poland, no one in Spain. She has never known hunger. Never. A blessed generation.

Her sons too have been blessed. They have turned out to be energetic young men deeply involved in independent projects of making successes of their lives. If they ever wailed in the night, it was because of nappy rash, or out of simple petulance, not because they were starving.

In their drive for success, her sons take after their father, not their mother. Their father has made an indubitable success of his life. As for their mother, one cannot yet be sure. Is it enough to have propelled two such well-fed, energetic young male beings into the world?

13. She is an intelligent person, well educated, well read, a good wife and mother. But she is not taken seriously. Nor is Margarita. Nor is the rest of their Circle. Society ladies: it is not difficult to make fun of them. Mocked for their good works. Mocked by themselves too. What a risible fate! Would she ever have guessed that it awaited her?

Perhaps that is why Margarita has chosen to fall ill today of all days. *¡Basta!* Enough of good works!

14. Her own husband keeps his distance from the Concert Circle. He believes in separate spheres of activity. A wife's sphere of activities should be her own.

They have grown apart, she and her husband. They were students together; he was her first love. In those early days they had a great passion for each other, insatiable. That passion persisted even after the birth of the children. Then one day it was no longer there. He had had enough. She too. Nonetheless she has remained a faithful wife. Men make passes at her, which she evades, not because they are unwelcome but because she has not taken the step yet, the step that is hers alone to take, the step from No to Yes.

15. She has her first sight of the Pole, in the flesh, when he strides onto the platform, takes a bow, and seats himself at the Steinway.

Born in 1943, therefore seventy-two years old. He moves easily; he does not look his age.

She is struck by how tall he is. Not just tall but big too, with a chest that seems about to burst out of his jacket. Crouched over the keyboard, he looks like a huge spider.

Hard to imagine great hands like that coaxing anything sweet and gentle out of a keyboard. Yet they do.

Do male pianists have an inborn advantage over women: hands that on a woman would look grotesque?

She has not given much thought to hands before, hands that do everything for their owners like obedient, unpaid servants. Her own hands are nothing special. The hands of a woman who will soon be fifty. Sometimes she discreetly hides them. Hands betray one's age, as does one's throat, as do the folds of one's armpit.

In her mother's day, a woman could still appear in public wearing gloves. Gloves, hats, veils: last traces of a vanished epoch.

16. The second thing that strikes her about the Pole is his hair, which is extravagantly white, extravagantly waved in a crest. Is that how he prepares for a recital, she wonders: seated with a hairdresser in his hotel room having his coiffure attended to? But perhaps she is ungenerous. Among maestros of his generation, the

heirs of the Abbé Liszt, a mane of hair, grey or white, must be standard equipment.

Years later, when the episode of the Pole has receded into history, she will wonder about those early impressions. She believes, on the whole, in first impressions, when the heart delivers its verdict, either reaching out to the stranger or recoiling from him. Her heart did not reach out to the Pole when she saw him stride onto the platform, toss back his mane, and address the keyboard. Her heart's verdict: *What a poseur! What an old clown!* It would take her a while to overcome that first, instinctive response, to see the Pole in his full selfhood. But what does *full selfhood* mean, really? Did the Pole's full selfhood not perhaps include being a poseur, an old clown?

17. The evening's recital falls into two halves. The first half consists of a Haydn sonata and a suite of dances by Lutosławski. The second half is given over to Chopin's twenty-four Preludes.

He plays the Haydn sonata with clean, crisp lines, as if to demonstrate that big hands need not be clumsy hands, but on the contrary can dance together as delicately as a lady's.

The little pieces by Lutosławski are new to her. They remind her of Bartók, of his peasant dances. She likes them.

She likes them more than the Chopin that follows. The Pole may have made a name as an interpreter of Chopin, but the Chopin she knows is more intimate and more subtle than what he offers. Her Chopin has the power to transport her out of the Barri Gòtic, out of Barcelona, into the drawing room of a great old country house in the remote Polish plains, with a long summer's day wheeling to an end, a breeze stirring the curtains, and the scent of roses wafting indoors.

To be transported, to be lost in transports: an outdated idea, in all likelihood, of what music does for its listeners—outdated and probably sentimental too. But that is what she desires on this particular evening, and that is what the Pole does not provide.

The applause, after the last of the Preludes, is polite but not enthusiastic. She is not the only one who came to hear Chopin played by a real Pole, and has been disappointed.

As an encore, as a gesture to his hosts, he offers a short piece by Mompou, played in a rather abstracted way, then with nary a smile is gone from the stage.

Does he happen to be in a bad mood today or is he always like this? Is he going to call home and complain about his reception at the hands of the philistine Catalans? Is there a Madame Pole back at home to hear his complaints? He does not look like a married man. He looks like a man with messy divorces behind him, and ex-wives grinding their teeth, wishing him ill.

18. The Pole, it turns out, does not speak French. He does, however, speak English, after a fashion; as for her, Beatriz, after her two years at Mount Holyoke she is fluent in the language. The polyglot Lesinskis are therefore supernumerary. But welcome nonetheless, taking some of the hostly burden off her shoulders. Ester in particular. Ester may be old and bent, but she is as sharp as a pin.

19. They take him to the restaurant to which they routinely take performers, an Italian establishment called Boffini's with too much bottle-green velvet in its decor but with a dependable Milanese chef.

Once they are seated, Ester is the first to speak. 'It must be difficult, maestro, to come to earth after you have been in the clouds with your sublime music.'

The Pole inclines his head, neither agreeing nor disagreeing about the clouds where he has been. At close quarters it is less easy to conceal marks of age. There are pouches under his eyes; the skin of his throat sags; the backs of his hands are mottled.

Maestro. Best to get it over with quickly, the question of names. 'If I may,' she says: 'how shall we address you? We in Spain find Polish names difficult, as you must have realized by now. And we can't go on calling you *maestro* all evening.'

'My name is Witold,' he says. 'You can call me Witold. Please.'

'And I am Beatriz. Our friends are Ester and Tomás.'

The Pole raises an empty glass to his three new friends: Ester, Tomás, Beatriz.

'I am sure, Witold,' says Ester, 'I am not the first to confuse you with that famous Swedish actor, you must know whom I mean.'

The ghost of a smile crosses the Pole's face. 'Max von Sydow,' he says. 'My bad brother. He follows me wherever I go.'

Ester is right: the same long, lugubrious face, the same faded blue eyes, the same erect posture. But the voice is disappointing. It lacks the bad brother's deep-throated resonance.

20. 'Tell us about Poland, Witold,' says Ester. 'Tell us why your countryman Frédéric Chopin chose to live in France rather than in his homeland.'

'If Chopin had lived longer he would have returned to Poland,' replies the Pole, managing the tenses warily but correctly. 'He was a young man when he departed, he was a young man when he died. Young men are not happy at home. They search adventure.'

'And you?' says Ester. 'Were you, like him, unhappy in your home country when you were a young man?'

It is an opportunity for the Pole, Witold, to tell them about what it was like to be young and restless in his unhappy homeland, about his yearning to escape to the decadent but exciting West, but he does not take it. 'Happiness is not the most important...the most important sentiment,' he says. 'Anyone can be happy.'

Anyone can be happy but it takes someone extraordinary to be unhappy, someone extraordinary like me—is that what he wants them to infer? She hears herself speak. 'What then is the most important sentiment, Witold? If happiness is not important, what is important?'

There is silence around the table. She catches Ester and her husband in a quick exchange of glances. *Is she going to make things difficult? These difficult hours that stretch before us—is she going to make them even more difficult?*

'I am a musician,' says the Pole. 'For me music is most important.'

He is not answering her question, he is deflecting it, but no matter. What she would like to ask, but does not, is: *What of Madame Witold? How does she feel when her husband says that happiness is not important? Or is there no Madame—did Madame run away long ago to find happiness in another's arms?*

21. He does not speak of Madame Witold but does speak of a daughter who had a training in music, then moved to Germany to sing in a band and did not come back. 'I went to hear her once. In Düsseldorf. It was good. She has a good voice. Good voice, good control, not so good music.'

'Yes, the young...' says Ester. 'They bring us such heartache. Still, it must be nice for you—nice to know that the musical line is being continued. And your country—how are affairs in your country nowadays?

I remember the good Pope, he was from there, was he not? John Paul.'

On the subject of John Paul the good Pope, the Pole seems reluctant to be drawn. She, Beatriz, does not regard John Paul as a good pope. Not even as a good man. He struck her from the beginning as a schemer, a politician.

22. They speak of the young Japanese violinist who was last month's visitor. 'Extraordinary technique,' says Tomás. 'It commences very early in Japan, the education for music. Two years old, three years old, the child carries a violin with him everywhere. To the toilet too! It is part of the body, like another arm, arm number three. At what age did you commence, maestro?'

'My mother was a singer,' says the Pole, 'so always in the house I was hearing music. My mother was my first teacher. Then another teacher, then to the academy in Kraków.'

'So you have always been a pianist. From a child.'

Gravely the Pole considers the word *pianist*. 'I have been a man who plays piano,' he says at last. 'Like the man who punches tickets in the bus. He is a man and he punches tickets, but he is not a ticket man.'

So in Poland, in the buses, they still have men who punch tickets—they have not been rationalized away. Maybe that is why young Witold did not run away to Paris, like his musical hero. Because in Poland they have men who punch tickets and men who play the piano. For the first time she warms to him. *Behind that solemn air*, she thinks to herself, *he may just possibly be a joker. Just possibly*.

23. 'You should try the veal,' says Tomás. 'The veal is always good here.'

The Pole demurs. 'In the evening I do not have a big stomach,' he says. He orders a salad followed by gnocchi with pesto.

A big stomach: might that be a Polish idiom? He certainly does not have a big stomach. He is even a bit— she reaches for a word she does not often have a need for—*cadavérico*, cadaverous. A man like that should bequeath his body to a medical school. They would appreciate having such big bones to practise their skills on.

Chopin was buried in Paris, but then afterwards, if she remembers correctly, some patriotic organization or other had him exhumed and transported back to the land of his birth. A tiny body, no weight at all. Tiny bones. Is such a tiny man big enough, great enough, to devote one's whole life to—a dreamer, when all is said and done, a weaver of elegant sonic fabrics? A serious question, to her mind.

Compared to Chopin, compared even to Witold his disciple, she does not of course count as a serious person. She knows that and accepts it. But surely she is entitled to know whether the hours she spends listening patiently to the tinkling of piano keys or the scraping of horsehair on gut, when she could be out on the streets feeding the poor, are not hours wasted but form part of a grander, richer design. *Speak!* she wants to say to the Pole. *Justify your art!*

24. Of course the man has no idea of what is going on inside her. To him she is part of the burden he has to bear for the sake of his career as a performer: one of those nagging wealthy women who will not leave him in peace until they have extorted their gram of flesh. At this very moment, in his correct but slow English, he is relating a story of the kind he presumes a woman like her wants to hear, a story about his first piano teacher, who sat over him with a *férula* and rapped him on the wrist whenever he made a mistake.

25. 'And now you must reveal to us, Witold,' says Ester: 'of all the cities of the world that you visit, which are you fondest of? Where—outside Barcelona, of course—do you get the warmest reception?'

Without allowing the Pole his chance to reply, to reveal which of the cities of the world is his favourite, she, Beatriz, cuts in. 'Before you tell us that, Witold, can we for a moment go back to Chopin? Why does Chopin live on, do you think? Why is he so important?'

The Pole inspects her coolly. 'Why is he important? Because he tells us about ourselves. About our desires. Which are sometimes not clear to us. That is my opinion. Which are sometimes desires for that which we cannot have. That which is beyond us.'

'I don't understand.'

'You do not understand because I do not explain well in English, not in any language, even in Polish. To understand you must be silent and listen. Let the music speak, then you will understand.'

She is not satisfied. The fact is, she listened this evening, listened intently, and did not like what she heard. If the Lesinskis were not there, if she were alone with the man, she would press him harder. *It is not Chopin who fails to speak to me, Witold, but* your *Chopin, the Chopin who uses* you *as his medium*—that is what she would say. *Claudio Arrau—you know him?*—she would go on—*Arrau remains, for me, a better interpreter, a better medium. Through Arrau, Chopin speaks to my heart. But of course Arrau was not from Poland, so perhaps there was something he was deaf to, some feature of the mystery of Chopin that foreigners will never understand.*

26. The evening has run its course. On the sidewalk outside Boffini's the Lesinskis take their leave ('Such a privilege, maestro!'). It is left to her to conduct the Pole back to his hotel.

Side by side in the taxi, talked out, they sit in silence. *What a day!* she thinks. She cannot wait to get into bed.

She is all too conscious of his smell, the smell of male sweat and eau de Cologne. Of course it is always hot on the platform under the lights. And the effort, the physical effort, of hitting all those keys, one after the other, in the correct order! So perhaps the smell can be excused. But still...

They arrive at the hotel. 'Good night, gracious lady,' says the Pole. He takes her hand and squeezes it. 'Thank you. Thank you too for your profound questions. I will not forget.' Then he is gone.

She inspects her hand. After its brief rest under that giant paw it seems smaller than usual. But unharmed.

27. A week after his departure a package arrives at the concert hall, addressed to her, with German postage stamps. It contains a CD—his recording of the Chopin Nocturnes—and a note in English: 'To the angel who watched over me in Barcelona. I pray that the music will speak to her. Witold.'

28. Does she like this man, Witold? Perhaps she does, on balance. She is sorry, mildly sorry, that she will not see him again. She likes the way he stands straight, sits up straight. She likes his attentiveness, the seriousness with which he listens to her when she speaks. *The woman with the profound questions*: she is glad he acknowledged that. And she is amused by his English, with its correct grammar and faulty idioms. What does she dislike about him? A number of things. Above all his dentures, too gleaming, too white, too fake.

TWO

1. She sleeps well that night. In the morning she plunges back into her routines. She promises herself she will find time to listen to the Pole's CD, but then forgets.

Months later an email pops up. How did he get her address? 'Esteemed lady, I am teaching master classes in Girona at the Conservatori Felip Pedrell. Your hospitality is not forgotten. May I offer you hospitality? If you will come to Girona I will be your host with pleasure. I will meet the train at any hour.' It is signed *Your friend Witold with the difficult name*.

She writes back. 'Dear Witold, Your friends in Barcelona remember your visit with pleasure. Thank you for the kind invitation. Unfortunately I am too busy at present to come to Girona. I wish you every success with your classes. Beatriz.'

She makes inquiries. What the man with the difficult name says is true: he is indeed giving piano classes in Girona. Why Girona, of all places? Surely he does not need the money.

The more she thinks about his return to Catalonia, the stranger it seems.

She writes a second email. 'Why are you here, Witold? Please be frank with me. I have no time for pretty lies. Beatriz.'

She deletes *I have no time for pretty lies* and sends the message. It is not just lies that she has no time for, but also circumlocutions, word games, veiled meanings.

His reply comes at once. 'I am here for you. I do not forget you.'

2. She allows a day to pass while she ruminates on *for you*. Whatever the words mean in English, whatever they mean in the Polish that presumably lies behind the English, what do they mean in reality? He is here for her as one is in a bakery for bread? And what does *here* mean anyway? What good does it do him if his *here* is Girona while hers is Barcelona? Or he is here for her as one is in a church for God?

3. When she was young she would unquestioningly follow impulses. She trusted her heart. *Yes*, said her heart. Or *No*. But (thank God!) she is no longer young. She is wiser, more prudent. She sees things as they are.

What does she see in the case of the Pole? She sees a man at the end of his career, driven by need or circumstance to take on a job that would once have been beneath him (the Conservatori Felip Pedrell is not a highly regarded institution), a man who, finding himself alone and lonely in a foreign town, makes a play for a woman he once crossed paths with. What would it say about her if she were to respond? More to the point, what does it say about her that the man expects she will respond?

4. Apart from her husband, she has no deep experience of men. But over the years she has given ear to numerous confessions and confidences from women friends. She has also with a cool eye observed how the men of her class behave. She has emerged from her explorations with no great respect for men and their appetites, no wish to have a wave of male passion splash over her.

She has never been a great traveller. Her husband finds her incurious. He is wrong. She is curious, deeply curious. But not about the wider world, and not about sex. What then is she curious about? About herself. About why, despite all, the thought of driving to Girona for the day tickles her fancy, makes her smile.

5. Without difficulty she finds her way to the Conservatori, a faceless building in the old part of the city. Its corridors are empty (it is early afternoon). Following a familiar melody, she opens a door marked Sala 1 and finds herself at the rear of a small auditorium. On the stage, at the piano, are the Pole and a young man. Noiselessly she slips into a seat. The students who make up the audience, thirty or so of them, pay her no attention.

They are working on the slow movement of Rachmaninov's second piano concerto. The young man embarks on the long, plaintive opening melody. The Pole lays a hand on his arm to halt him. 'La—la—la—la—la—la—la—*laa*,' he sings, prolonging the final *la*. '*No demasiado legato.*'

The young man tries the melody again, with less *legato*.

Wearing slacks and an open-neck shirt, the Pole looks more relaxed than she remembers him. *Good!* she thinks. *And he has picked up a few words of Spanish!* Though to teach music one does not need many words. *Sí. No.*

She has not heard him sing before. An unexpectedly deep voice, like a dark stream, liquid.

6. What interests her about the scene is not the music but the drama. Because they are on a stage, because there is an audience, teacher and pupil have perforce become actors. How does the young man respond to direction when perhaps he does not agree with it (perhaps his way of playing, with more *legato*, was close to his heart)? Does he submit or does he rebel? Or does he pretend to submit but secretly rebel, promising himself he will go back to the old way once the Pole has vanished from the scene? And what of the Pole? Does he play the role of autocrat or of fatherly adviser?

7. The Pole leans over and plays the broken chords that open the movement. In the voice of the clarinet, he sings: 'La—la—la—la—la—la—la—*laa*.' Then the right hand enters, and at once she hears the difference. Less *legato*, less emotion, more tension, more lift.

The young man follows, and this time gets it right. He is good. He learns quickly. The Pole nods. '*Continúe*.'

8. The lesson ends, the students drift away. She stays behind. The Pole approaches her. What will he say?

He takes her hand. He thanks her, in English, for

coming. He expresses his pleasure at seeing her again. He compliments her on the dress she is wearing. His compliments do not please her. They have a practised, rehearsed air. But perhaps he simply does not know how to sound easy in English. Perhaps back in Poland he is a perfectly charming gentleman.

She has dressed carefully for the occasion. That is to say, she has dressed soberly.

'Can we talk?' she says.

9. They go for a walk on a tree-lined path along the riverside. It is a pleasant autumn day. The leaves are turning, et cetera.

'I ask again,' she says: 'why have you come here? Girona—you have no reason to be in Girona.'

'We all have to be somewhere. We cannot be nowhere. That is the human condition. But no. I am here for you.'

'So you say, but what does it mean? What do you want from me? You did not invite me here to listen to your piano classes. Do you want me to sleep with you? If so, let me tell you at once: it is not going to happen.'

'Do not be angry,' he says. 'Please.'

'I am not angry. I am impatient. I don't have time for games. You invited me here. Why?'

Why is she so angry? What does she want from him that he is refusing to give?

'Dear lady,' says the Pole, 'you remember Dante Alighieri the poet? His Beatrice never gave him one word and he loved her all his life.'

Dear lady!

'And is that why I am here: to be informed that you plan to love me all your life?'

'My life is not so long,' says the Pole.

Poor fool! she wants to say. *You come too late, the feast is over.*

She shakes her head. 'We are strangers, you and I,' she says. 'We belong to different worlds, different realms. You belong in one world with your Dante and your Beatrice, I belong in another, which I am accustomed to call the real world.'

'You give me peace,' says the Pole. 'You are my symbol of peace.'

She, Beatriz, a symbol of peace! She has never heard anything more nonsensical.

10. They walk on. The river flows softly, a breeze blows, the footpath stretches before them. Details, incidental yet not unimportant. Step by step her mood lightens.

'When you were teaching your student you sang,' she says. 'I had never thought of you as a singer. You have a good voice.'

'From my mother I am a singer. From my mother I am a musician.'

A mother's boy. Is that what he is in quest of: mothering?

Time is getting short. Either he must begin to plead his cause or she will get in her car and drive home and that will be the end of it. It is time for his grand aria. He must sing: that is her demand. In Italian, in Spanish, in English, it does not matter which. Even in Polish.

'Dear lady,' says the Pole, 'I am not a poet. I can only say, since I met you my memory is full of you, the image of you. I travel from one city to another city to another city, that is my job, but always you are with me. You protect me. I have peace inside me. I say to myself, I must find her, she is my destiny. Therefore I am here. And with such joy to see you!'

She gives him peace. She gives him joy. Not much of an aria. Also, his destiny has been revealed to him, and she is it. But what about her? Does she not have a destiny too? What might that destiny be? When will it be revealed?

11. She has no reason to disbelieve him when he says that because of her, because of a chance invitation that brought him to Barcelona, he now has intervals of peace and joy. He bears her image with him as a lover in the old days bore the image of his sweetheart in a locket around his neck. Very pretty. If she were young, if he were young, she might be flattered. But from a man born in 1943, a man old enough to be her father, the bid he is making for her is neither amusing nor flattering. It is, if anything, distasteful.

'Listen to me, Witold,' she says. 'You barely know me, so let me tell you who I am. First and last, I am a married woman. Not a free spirit but a woman with a husband and children and a home and friends and commitments of all kinds, emotional commitments, social commitments, practical commitments. There is no room in my life for—what shall I call it?—an affair of the heart. You tell me you carry around with you an image of me. Good. But I don't carry around an image of you. I don't carry around an image of anyone. I am not that kind of person. You visited Barcelona, you gave a piano recital, which we all enjoyed; we had dinner together; and that was that. You passed into my life, you passed out of my life. *Terminado*. We have no future together, you and I. I am sorry to say so, but it is the truth. Now I think we should turn back. It is getting late.'

12. 'I will make a proposal,' says the Pole.

They are sitting in a café across the street from where her car is parked.

'Next month I go on a tour to America. After America I go to Brazil. I have three concerts there. Do you know Brazil? No? Perhaps you will come to Brazil with me.'

'You want me to come to Brazil?'

'Yes. We will have a vacation. Do you like the sea? We can have our vacation next to the sea.'

She likes the sea, likes it very much. She is a good swimmer, strong in the water, like a seal. Strong and agile. But that is not the question.

'And what shall I say to my husband?' she says. 'That I am going off to Brazil with a man I barely know? And you? What do you plan to say to your wife? You have never told me—are you married?'

He sets down his cup; his hand quivers noticeably. Does she make him nervous? Is he about to tell a lie?

'No, I am not married. Once I was married, but now,

no. Say to your husband the truth. The truth is always good. He is a man of affairs. He is free, you are free.'

'You astonish me. You know nothing about my husband. My husband is not "a man of affairs". Nor am I a woman of affairs. And let me tell you, for use in the future, this is not how a man goes about luring a woman into going off to Brazil with him. Perhaps it works in Poland, but not here. I must go now. I have a long drive ahead of me.'

She rises. It is the Pole's last chance. He too rises, to his full and considerable height, grips her by the shoulders. The people at the next table glance across: are they going to witness a domestic quarrel? She pulls free of his grasp. 'I really must go.'

13. On the highway, near the turnoff to Malgrat, she passes a crash site: a tangle of metal, police cars, an ambulance. She shivers. *What if that had been me? What would people say? 'What was she doing in Girona?'*

What was she doing in Girona indeed? Already it seems like an aberration: answering the call of a man whose name she cannot spell. Answering his call, but then recovering herself, thank God! *Come with me to Brazil*. What nonsense!

14. She speaks to her husband. 'I don't know if you remember, but some months ago we had a pianist from Poland at the Concert Circle. It turns out he is now in Girona, giving classes at the conservatorium. He invited me there.'

'Yes? And you will go?'

'I was there this afternoon. He wants me to come with him to Brazil. He has fallen in love with me. So he says.'

'And will you go?'

'Of course not. I am just telling you.'

Why is she telling him? So that she can draw a line under the story. So that her conscience can be clean.

'Are you jealous?' she says.

'Of course I am jealous. I would be jealous of any man who fell in love with you.'

But he is not jealous. She can see that. He is, if anything, amused: amused that another man should aspire to what belongs to him alone, to what he owns so easily.

'Will you see him again?' says her husband.

'No,' she says. And then: 'It is not about sex.'

'Of course it is about sex. Why else do you think he has invited you to Brazil? To sit by his side and turn the pages of his piano score?'

15. From the Pole arrives a long letter, whose surface she skims. Peace seems to be the key word. She brings him peace. Peace as opposed to what? War? What does he know about war, sitting in front of a piano all day, lost in the clouds?

Ahead of her she catches a glimpse of the B word, *Brazil*. Without reading further, she deletes the letter.

16. She is incurious about her husband's affairs, deliberately so. In return, he is careful not to involve himself with women from their own social circle. That is the modus vivendi they have arrived at, and it has served them well.

17. Another email from the Pole. Today is his last day in Girona, he will be passing through Barcelona tomorrow on his way to the airport for a flight to Berlin. Will she have lunch with him? 'Sorry, no time,' she writes back. 'Travel safely. Beatriz.'

18. She resurrects the CD he sent her, brings home the Walczykiewicz CDs from the Concert Circle's little library, and listens to them in solitude. Why? Because she is prepared to entertain the idea that what the man

cannot express in his bare-bones English he may be able to express through his art.

She starts with the Nocturnes. What was Chopin saying to the world when he dreamed up his Nocturnes? More important, what was the Pole saying to the world on the day he made the recording? Most important of all, what might the Pole, on the day he made the recording, have been revealing of himself to a woman of whose existence in the real world he had as yet no inkling?

As before, she is disappointed. She finds herself chilled by—what shall she call it?—the style, the approach, the mentality of the interpreter. So dry, so matter-of-fact! Each piece held up for inspection, examined, then, with the final chord, folded away and interred.

Perhaps the truth is that, even at the time when he made the recording (she checks the notes on the CD: 2009, they say), the Pole was too old in spirit for music like this, music that belongs to more ardent souls.

Something to do with touch. She recalls the touch of his hand in the taxi on the evening they met; she recalls the touch of his lips to her cheek when he greeted her in Girona. Like being touched by dry bone. A living skeleton. She shivers. She too has a skeleton, but unlike his hers is ghostly, impalpable.

Is that, then, her final verdict on him: too dry, too lacking in ardour? Is that what she wants in a man: ardour? If ardour were to arrive tomorrow, out of the blue, and announce itself—real, impetuous ardour—would there be room for it in her life? She doubts it.

19. Of all the music he has recorded, it is the mazurkas that she likes best. He comes most alive when he joins his master in these country dances. Strange: she does not think of him as a dancer.

20. Perhaps, after all, the fault does not lie wholly with the Pole, the two Poles—the young one long dead, the old one still current. Perhaps she carries a share of the blame. All that she seems to like in music nowadays is song and dance, not drama with its ups and downs (*forte! piano! forte! piano!*) and certainly not philosophizing. Music that spends its time questing after a lost object (Mahler) makes her yawn. That is why the Pole himself does not interest her, in the end. Roaming the world in search of his own lost object, he has chanced upon her, Beatriz, and turned her into a fetish. *You*

bring me peace: what nonsense! *I am not the answer to the riddle of your life, Señor Witold—your riddle or anyone else's!* That is what she should have said to him. *I am who I am!*

21. For years she and her husband have not shared a bedroom. The arrangement suits them both. She likes to go to bed early after a hot bath, whereas he likes to stay up late. She sleeps better alone, and so perhaps does he. She sleeps eight hours a night, sometimes nine. She sleeps deeply, nourishingly.

She and her husband are no longer intimate. She is getting used to doing without sex. She does not seem to need it. Her climacteric has not yet arrived, but is on its way. Then she will cease to be fruitful, and the body's faint cry for union will die away.

22. Her friends have love affairs but she does not. Her friend Margarita is having an affair with a well-known professor of anthropology, a media celebrity, a married man. They meet in hotels or in an apartment belonging to an obliging colleague.

23. She has visited Argentina but never Brazil. She

would not mind seeing Brazil. It seems an interesting country. Perhaps her elder son, who works as a chemist for an agronomics company, would find it useful to accompany her there. He could explore Brazilian agriculture.

24. She has no intention of going to Brazil in the company of the Polish pianist. Anyway, if she were to go, how would he explain her to his Brazilian hosts—to the Brazilian equivalent of her Concert Circle? 'This is Beatriz, an old friend from the city of Barcelona, who is accompanying me on my tour. Beatriz has long wanted to see your infinitely various country.' Or: 'This is Beatriz, whom I have brought with me to soothe my brow and give me peace.' Or: 'This is Beatriz, a woman I barely know but who seems to be the answer to the riddle of why I exist.'

25. An old man in love. Foolish. And a danger to himself.

26. He had his chance when he gripped her by the shoulders in the café in Girona and thrust his face at her, his cold blue eyes. That was the moment for him

to make his mark on her, to overbear her resistance. But he faltered and lost her.

27. She dislikes the Portuguese language, with its tight, choked sounds. But perhaps the Portuguese spoken in Brazil is different.

28. She thinks of how it would be to share a bed with that huge bony frame, and shivers with distaste. Those cold hands on her body.

29. Why her? What happened, during the evening they spent over dinner at Boffini's, that made him think, *This is my destiny! This is a woman on whom I must spend my last love*? If Margarita had not been ill that day but had been one of the party, would he have fallen for Margarita instead, and would Margarita now be the one invited to Brazil to soothe his brow and share his bed?

Peace: that is what he says he wants. As a storm-tossed navigator prays for landfall, so he prays for peace. Well, Margarita is no angel of peace, as he would soon discover. Margarita would fit him out with new, more modish clothes, take him to her *esteticista* to have his eyebrows attended to, fix him up with media interviews. As for sex, would he, at his age, be able to perform to Margarita's demanding standard?

Perhaps, if the truth be told, that is why he settled on her, Beatriz. Because in his line of work he comes across too many women like Margarita, energetic, brilliant, acquisitive; because, that evening at Boffini's, she, Beatriz, seemed the epitome of the unobtrusive, undemanding yet entirely presentable woman who would attend to his needs without giving too much trouble. If so, what an insult!

30. She writes a letter to him, in English: 'Dear Witold, I trust that your concert in Berlin went well. I have been reflecting on our last conversation, wondering how on earth you came to the conclusion that I am the embodiment of peace. I embody neither peace nor anything else. The fact is, you know nothing of who or what I am. Your path crossed mine by the purest of chance. There was no design behind it. I was not meant for you, as you seem to think. I was not "meant" for anyone. None of us is "meant", whatever the word means. Yours, Beatriz.'

31. Between a man and a woman, between the two

poles, electricity either crackles or does not crackle. So it has been since the beginning of time. A man *and* a woman, not just a man, a woman. Without *and* there is no conjunction. Between herself and the Pole there is no *and*.

Next month's visitor to the Concert Circle will be the counter-tenor Thomas Kirchwey, who will present a program of Handel, Pergolesi, Philip Glass and someone named Martynov whom she has never heard of. Perhaps Thomas Kirchwey will turn out to be her true pole, eclipsing the false Pole, the pretender.

32. She rereads her letter, decides that it sounds too angry, deletes it. Why does it sound angry? She did not feel angry when she wrote it.

33. His idol Chopin was a sickly man who relied on a woman to look after him. Perhaps that is what the Pole really wants: a nurse to take care of him in his declining years.

34. 'That pianist you told me about, the one with the long name,' says her husband—'have you made up your mind yet?'

'Made up my mind about what?'

'Will you be going with him to Brazil?'

'Of course not. Whatever made you think I would?'

'Does he know you will not be coming with him?'

'Of course he does. I made it clear to him.'

'Does he call you? Does he write to you? Are you and he in correspondence?'

'In correspondence? No, we are not. And I am not answering any more questions. Don't you find this a strange conversation for the two of us to be having—a civilized married couple?'

35. Now there are two puzzles to solve: why her mind keeps going back to the Pole; and why her husband has turned hostile.

The second is the easier to answer. Her husband has sniffed something in the air and is reacting. It is a matter of psychology, nothing more.

The first is not a matter of psychology. It is a matter of missing things, and for missing things there seems to be, as yet, no ology. Mysterology? Mysterics?

36. Two images of Brazil come to her mind's eye,

two stereotypes: bronzed bodies lazing on beaches of dazzling whiteness; and women with wailing babies sweating over gas stoves in leaky shacks. Of course that is not all of Brazil. A third Brazil, a fourth Brazil, a hundredth Brazil await the visitor.

37. Brazil does not represent a crisis in her marriage. There is no crisis in her marriage. She has no intention of leaving her husband; and her husband would be a fool if he left her. She is not in love with the Pole. At most she is sorry for him: sorry for his being lonely and old and out of touch with a world that is less and less receptive to his at-a-distance renderings of Chopin. Sorry for him too for his fixation on her (he may call it love but she does not).

38. Brazil in his company would be impossible. How would they spend their time when he is not playing Chopin to Brazilian high society? Taking walks on long white beaches amid bronzed Brazilian bodies? Dancing to Brazilian bands?

She likes familiar things. She likes being comfortable. She dislikes novelty for the sake of novelty. No wonder her husband finds her incurious.

Martynov, for example. She has never heard of Martynov, therefore she is ready to dislike his music. It does not reflect well on her.

39. Why is she castigating herself, making herself look foolish and complacent and even philistine? What has got into her?

40. She does not dream. She never dreams. She sleeps long and deeply and dreamlessly, and wakes in the morning refreshed, renewed. With her restful sleep and healthy way of life she will probably live to be a hundred.

Instead of dreaming she indulges her imagination. She can imagine all too well what a week in Brazil in the company of the Pole would be like. In particular she can imagine what it would be like if they slept together. She would have to pretend to be in ecstasies and he would have to pretend to believe her.

I absolve you: that is what she needs to say to him before they set foot on Brazilian soil. *I absolve you from all erotic duties. You sleep in your bed and I will sleep in mine.*

41. She wonders if he keeps a diary. *Diary of a Seducer*.

Would he dare to put her in his diary? The week he spent in Brazil with a certain lady from Barcelona, 'who out of respect for her family shall remain nameless'.

THREE

1. An email arrives with an audio file attached: Chopin's B minor sonata. 'I record this for you alone. In English I cannot say what is in my heart, therefore I say it in music. Please listen, I pray to you.'

She obeys. She listens, paying hawk-like attention to the phrasing, the inflections, the minutest accelerations and decelerations—anything that could be construed as a private message. She comes up blank, baffled. It sounds just like his Deutsche Grammophon recording in the Concert Circle library. If he has smuggled in a message, it is in a code she does not know how to read.

2. Time passes. Another email: 'I will be in Mallorca in October for the Chopin festival. After Mallorca, perhaps your concert circle will invite me again. That is my warm hope.'

She writes back: 'Dear Witold, Thank you for the recording, and how good to hear you will be playing at the Chopin festival. Alas, the program of our

Concert Circle is settled for the rest of the year. Yours, Beatriz.'

A day later she writes again. 'Dear Witold, It so happens that my husband's family owns a house near the town of Sóller, not far from Valldemossa, where the Chopin festival will be held. My husband and I will be spending some time there in October. Would you like to join us after your commitments? The house is spacious. You will have your own quarters. Let me know what you think. Yours, Beatriz.'

He writes back: 'Thank you, thank you, but I cannot be a friend of the family. Witold.' He adds a PS: '*A Friend of the Family* is a famous Polish novel. People call it the Polish *Werther*.'

She has heard of *Werther* but not of *A Friend of the Family*. Is there another coded message here? Does he expect her to track down *A Friend of the Family* and read it? Absurd man!

3. She speaks to her husband. 'Are we still going to Sóller in October?'

'Yes, if you like, if the house is free.'

'The house will be free. I thought of asking Tomás and Eva and the child.'

'Good! Good! Will you make the arrangements? But not for longer than a week.'

'I will make the arrangements, but I will probably stay on after you leave. A week is too short.'

She is not often duplicitous. She prefers frankness. She prefers laying her cards on the table. But sometimes laying one's cards on the table is not a good idea.

4. She speaks to Tomás, her son. 'Not possible,' he says. 'I can't take time off from work, and anyway it's no fun travelling with a baby.'

5. She books flights and calls the housekeeper in Sóller to instruct her to open up the house.

She enjoys making plans, settling details. If the Concert Circle runs smoothly, it is due to her diligence and her care for detail.

6. She has no intention of going to Valldemossa to hear the Pole play. Let him come to her.

Plotting. Plotting.

7. The house outside Sóller was bought during the 1940s by her husband's grandfather, who had made his

fortune in shipping. At the time when he bought it, it was still the hub of a working farm, but over the years he sold off the farmland parcel by parcel, until he was left with only the big house and its outbuildings.

It was there that her husband spent his holidays as a child, and he still has a deep attachment to the place. He is deeply attached yet he visits less and less, she cannot understand why. She herself has come to love the old house, with its austere stonework and its high ceilings and its dim passages and the cool courtyard with its riot of plumbago and bougainvillea and the great old fig tree at its centre.

8. There is the question of conscience. Is her conscience going to plague her over her invitation to the Pole? Her conscience did not plague her over the young man at the gymnasium whom she allowed to flirt with her last year and who once cornered her and tried to kiss her (she yielded her neck, her throat, but not her lips). Is it a question of territory? Is the gymnasium neutral ground whereas the house in Sóller is her husband's territory and the territory of his family going back two generations?

The Pole is in his seventies, in the evening of his

years. The man at the gymnasium was in his twenties, with a vigorous male life stretching before him. The cases are hardly comparable. It would be forgivable if her husband were jealous of the man at the gymnasium but not if he were jealous of the Pole. A man of the Pole's age should not give rise to jealousy, he does not have that power. In any event, she has no intention of sleeping with him. When he comes to Sóller he can share her domestic routines. He can accompany her to the supermarket and help carry the groceries. He can dredge leaves out of the swimming pool. There is a piano in one of the spare rooms, an old upright: he can fix it up and play for her. By the end of the week his romantic fantasies will have gone up in smoke. He will have seen her as she truly is. He can then return to his native land a sadder and a wiser man.

9. 'Do you remember the Polish pianist who asked me to fly with him to Brazil?' she says to her husband. 'He is going to be in Mallorca at the same time as we are. He will be performing at the Chopin festival. Do you mind if I invite him to lunch?'

'Of course not. But wouldn't you rather see him by yourself?'

'No, I think he should see me *en famille*. That should bring him down to earth. He has rather elevated notions about me.'

Plotting.

10. Her invitation to the Pole is couched in unusually specific terms. If he wishes to see her, he should plan to arrive on such-and-such a date and depart on such-and-such a date. He should catch the number 203 bus from Valldemossa to the bus station in Sóller. If he calls in advance and informs her of his time of arrival, she will pick him up. He will be housed not in the main residence but in a cottage on the grounds. The cottage has a fully equipped kitchen, in case he wishes to cook for himself. Otherwise he is welcome to share meals with her, Beatriz, his hostess, meals which will be prepared by the housekeeper. His time will be his own.

It reads, and is meant to read, like an invitation to a paying guest.

11. When the time comes, she and her husband travel to Sóller and enjoy a quiet week together. The weather is a little cool, a little windy, but nothing to complain about. The roads are empty, most of the tourists are

gone. They drive to Banyalbufar, to Peguera, where she has a long, invigorating swim. They dine at a restaurant in Fornalutx that they have always been fond of.

12. 'What has happened about the Polish musician?' asks her husband. 'I thought he was coming to lunch.'

'The dates didn't work out,' she replies. 'He isn't free until next week, and you will be gone by then.'

'What a pity,' says her husband. 'I would have liked to meet him.'

He smiles. She smiles. They have navigated tricky passages before, they will navigate this one.

13. Her husband leaves. The Pole arrives. She picks him up at the bus station in the little Suzuki that they keep in Sóller. Nearly a year has passed since Girona. He has noticeably aged. He is in fact an old man.

Of course it is natural that he should have aged. Why should he be proof against the ravages of time? Nevertheless she is disappointed—more than disappointed, dismayed.

She wonders what the audiences in Valldemossa thought of him. *A spectre from the past*—is that what they thought? But perhaps, for some, he assumes an aura of timeless authority when he sits down at the keyboard.

14. He kisses her on both cheeks. 'So fresh you look, so beautiful,' he murmurs. His lips are dry, his skin soft, babyish: the skin of an old man.

15. They drive to the house in silence. The road up the hill is pitted, but she is a good driver, better than most of the men she knows. When they are on the island her husband leaves the driving to her. 'I know I am in safe hands,' he says.

16. She shows the Pole to his cottage. 'I will leave you to unpack and settle in. When lunch is ready Loreto will ring the bell.'

'You are gracious,' says the Pole.

Gracious: what an old-fashioned, bookish word. Does it have a meaning any longer? *Ave Maria, gratia plena, ora pro nobis.*

17. He responds promptly to the lunchtime bell. He has changed his clothes. He now wears sandals, cream-coloured slacks, a sky-blue shirt. He bears a Panama hat, ready for what the afternoon will bring.

She introduces him to Loreto. *No habla español*, she tells Loreto. He doesn't speak Spanish. Loreto gives him a tight smile, a nod. *Señor*.

Loreto looks after this house and another, further down the valley, belonging to a Mexican. She arrives and leaves on a 125 cc moped. Her husband is an odd-job man and gardener. They have a son and a daughter, both grown up, both married, both living on the mainland.

Nothing about Loreto is surprising. That is to say, of what she knows about Loreto nothing surprises her, not even the moped. But of course Loreto has a life of her own, invisible to her employers, which may well be full of surprises. It may contain, for instance, Loreto's equivalent of the Pole: a man who finds her, Loreto, to be full of grace and worth pursuing. It is only a matter of chance that the story being told is not about Loreto and her man but about her, Beatriz, and her Polish admirer. Another fall of the dice and the story would be about Loreto's submerged life.

18. 'I hope you are hungry. Loreto has made us old-style *tumbet*. Do you know it? Did they serve it in Valldemossa? In Catalonia we have a similar dish but we call it *samfaina*.'

She has always been a good hostess, skilled at putting guests at their ease. It is particularly important to put the Pole at his ease, to make him feel at home, so that when he leaves it will be with pleasant memories.

'Your husband did not come?' says the Pole.

'My husband came, but then was called back to his office. He sends his regrets. He is sorry he could not meet you.'

'He is a good man, your husband?'

What a strange question. 'Yes, I believe he is a good man. It is not hard to be good, in our times.'

'Yes? You think so?'

'I do. We live in fortunate times. In fortunate times it is not hard to be good. Do you think otherwise?'

'I do not live in fortunate times. But I try to be good.'

She does not see how the person sitting on one side of the table can live in fortunate times while the person on the other side of the table does not, but she lets it pass. 'Tell me about your daughter the singer. She lives in Germany, I remember you saying. How is she getting on?'

'I will show you.' He takes out his phone and shows her a picture of a tall, serious-looking girl in her teens dressed all in white. 'It is an old picture, from the old days, but I keep it. Now it is different. She is married, she lives in Berlin, she and her husband have a restaurant, a grand success, which brings them much money. The singing? That is in the past, I think. So: successful, yes, but not happy. Not blessed.'

Not blessed. It is sometimes hard to know what the man means, with his incomplete English. Is he saying something profound or is he simply hitting the wrong words, like a monkey sitting in front of a typewriter? Are people with much money truly not happy? She has much money and is happy, more or less. The Pole must have much money too, after all his concerts, and does not seem unhappy. Gloomy perhaps, but not miserable. Perhaps he means that the daughter in Berlin is discontented. Discontent is not uncommon. Discontent: not knowing what one wants.

'Do you see her often? Do you and she get along together?'

The Pole raises his hands, palms upwards, in a gesture she cannot decode. Where she comes from it means *Have courage, press on!* but where he comes from it could mean something quite different—*There is nothing to be done*, for example.

'We are civilized,' says the Pole. 'But she does not have my soul. She has her mother's soul.'

Civilized. How to translate? *We do not fly at each other's throat? We do not yawn in each other's face? We greet each other with a kiss on the cheek?* Whatever the case, being civilized in each other's company does not seem much of an achievement for a father and daughter.

'Fortunately,' she says, 'my children and I share the same soul. The same dispositions. We have the same blood running in our veins.'

'That is good,' says the Pole.

'Yes, it is good. I invited my elder son to join us here in Sóller. He is a serious person. You would like him. Unfortunately, he could not come. He and his wife have a new baby, and his wife finds it a strain to travel. One can understand.'

'So you are a grandmother now.'

'Yes. I will be fifty on my next birthday. Were you aware of that?'

'A gentleman does not ask a lady's age.'

He delivers this pronouncement with a straight face. Does he never smile? Does he have no sense of the ridiculous?

'It sometimes happens,' she says, 'that what a gentleman does not ask of a lady turns out to be what the gentleman in question does not want to know about the lady. What the gentleman would find unpleasing to know. Because it would upset some of the ideas about the lady that the gentleman holds. Some of his preconceptions.'

The Pole breaks off a wedge of bread, dips it in the sauce, makes no reply. Loreto, in the far corner of the kitchen, pretends to be washing the pans, but her manner suggests that she is listening. Perhaps she knows more English than she lets on.

'Have you finished?' she says. 'Have you had enough? Would you like coffee?'

19. Loreto serves them coffee in the living room, where the huge windows (an innovation of her husband's) allow a view over the valley and its almond groves.

'So, Witold, here you are at last, in sunny Mallorca in the company of your elusive lady friend. Are you happy at last?'

'Dearest lady, I do not have the words. Not the words in English, not the words in any language. But gratitude, yes. Gratitude comes up from my heart, you can see it.' With two hands he makes a strange, awkward gesture, as if opening his ribcage from the bottom and lifting out the contents.

'I see it, I believe it. But your grand design still escapes me—your design, your plan. Why are you here, now that you are here? What do you want from your friend?'

'Dear lady, perhaps we can be like normal people and do normal things—no? Without a plan. A normal man and a normal woman do not have a plan.'

'Really? Do you think so? That is not my experience. In my experience normal men and normal women very often have plans relative to each other. Designs. But let us pretend we have no plan. Then let me ask: when you go back to Poland, and your friends say to you, "So you spent a week on the island of Mallorca with a lady friend! What was it like?" how will you reply? Will you say that it was okay, nothing out of the normal about it? That it was just like being in Poland except that the sun was shining?'

The Pole gives a laugh, a short, explosive burst. It is the first time she has heard him laugh. 'Always you push me in a corner,' he says. 'You know I am not clever like you in the English language. If not *normal*, what is a better word in English?'

'*Normal* is a good word. Nothing wrong with it.'

'*Ordinary*,' he says. 'Maybe *ordinary* is better. I wish

to live with you. That is the wish of my heart. I wish to live with you until I die. In an ordinary way. Side by side. So.' He clasps his hands tightly together. 'An ordinary life side by side—that is what I want. For always. The next life too, if there is another life. But if not, okay, I accept. If you say no, not for the rest of life, just for this week—okay, I accept that too. For just a day even. For just a minute. A minute is enough. What is time? Time is nothing. We have our memory. In memory there is no time. I will hold you in my memory. And you, maybe you will remember me too.'

'Of course I will remember you, you strange man.'

She utters the words without forethought, hears them echo startlingly in her mind's ear. What is she saying? How can she promise to remember him when she has every reason to believe that the episode of the Polish musician who paid her a visit in Sóller is going to fade and fade until on her deathbed it is less than a speck of dust?

The man seems to trust in the powers of memory. She would like to tell him about the powers of forgetting. How much has she not forgotten! And she is a normal person, an ordinary person, not an exception at all.

What has she forgotten? She has no idea. It is gone, has vanished from the face of the earth as if it had never existed.

20. She rouses herself. 'Shall we go for a walk?' she says. 'Have you brought walking shoes? The wind picks up in the late afternoon, so if we want to go it is best we go now.'

The Pole changes his shoes and they go for their walk, following a track that will take them to the crest of the hill overlooking the town. He is slow but not as slow as she feared he might be.

'What is Poland like?' she says. 'I have never been there, as you know.'

'Poland is not beautiful like this. Poland is full of rubbish. Centuries of rubbish. We do not bury it. We do not hide it. To love Poland you must be born there. You will not love my country, if you come.'

'But you love Poland.'

'I love Poland and I hate Poland. This is not special. For many Poles it is true.'

'Your master—Frédéric Chopin—left Poland and never went back. You could have done the same.'

'Yes, I could say goodbye to Poland and buy an

apartment in Valldemossa and wait for some French lady to arrive, some George Sand who is tired of French men with crude habits, who wants a gentle Pole to give her love to. Or I could find an apartment in Barcelona. But that would not be good for you, so I don't do it. It is the truth—no?'

Indeed, indeed! Indeed it is the truth! It would indeed not be good for her to have this man hovering at her doorstep, casting his shadow over her. 'I agree. It would be a very bad idea for you to be living in Barcelona. Bad for me and perhaps even worse for you.'

But why is he bringing up George Sand? Whatever he has in mind, she finds the thought distasteful: herself as his foreign mistress, his part-time nurse.

They have reached the crest. There they halt, gazing out over the coastline. Lovers would put their arms around each other. Lovers might even kiss. But not they.

'About this evening,' she says: 'would you like to go out or shall I cook for us? There are one or two good restaurants in Sóller. Or we could drive further afield.'

'The lady—Loreta is her name?—she does not cook for you?'

'Loreto does not come in every day. Also, her working day ends at three. If we want her to come back in the evening I will have to make a special arrangement.'

'Tonight I prefer we stay at home. Tomorrow I take you to a restaurant. But tonight we stay at home and I help you cook.'

'Very well, we stay at home. I cook, but you do not help.' She has a vision of the Pole in the kitchen, blundering around, knocking things over, getting in the way. 'I cook and you take a rest.' It is like talking to a child.

21. For supper she makes a big omelette with herbs from the garden, and a salad. She is determined that everything remain simple. If the man is still hungry there is always bread.

They have a good cellar here in Sóller. Stocking the cellar is her husband's department. She does not drink much; the Pole drinks more.

'I have a gift for you,' says the Pole.

She unties the ribbon, lifts the lid of the little box. Inside is what appears to be a pine cone.

'It is a rose,' he explains.

It is indeed a rose, carved with considerable delicacy in a blond wood.

'It's very pretty,' she says.

'It is from the house of the Chopins, the parents of Frédéric. It is folk art in Poland. Mainly this folk art is for religion, for the altar in the church. But the parents of Frédéric were not religious, so this was in the house for décor, with other flowers. In their time it was painted, but the paint is gone, it is two hundred years in the past, and to me it is more beautiful with just the wood. I don't know how you call the wood in English. In Polish it is świerk.'

So she is to become custodian of a relic of the sainted Chopin. Is she the right person for the job, who does not believe in God, much less in Chopin? 'Thank you, Witold,' she says. 'It is beautiful. I will treasure it. But I am going to say goodnight now. I go to bed early. It is not a very Spanish habit, but for me it is so. You will have to retire too, I am afraid. I have to lock the house, I cannot sleep easily if the house is not locked. I will leave a light on outside. Goodnight.' She presents her cheek to be kissed. 'Sleep well.'

22. Usually she falls asleep at once. But not tonight. Has she made a mistake, inviting the Pole to Sóller? *I want to live side by side with you like two clasped hands. In the*

next life too. What sentimental nonsense! *You give me peace.* And a rose from the home of his hero. *For you!* What a joke!

The rest of the week yawns before her. How are they going to occupy their time? With rambles? With idiot conversations? With visits to the beach, visits to restaurants? How much of such a routine can they bear—two polite, civilized, normal people—before one of them snaps? And this was supposed to be a vacation!

What does the man want? What does *she* want?

23. It is daytime. They have had breakfast.

'I have something to show you,' she says. She conducts him to one of the back rooms, where a piano has stood, covered with a dust sheet, for as long as she can remember.

She removes the sheet. 'Have a look at it,' she says. 'Is it any good?'

He shrugs. 'It is old,' he says. 'It is made in Spain. Spain is not famous for pianos.' He plays a scale. The keys are slow and sticky, a hammer is missing, the strings are badly out of tune. 'You have tools?'

'Piano tools? No.'

'Not piano tools, just tools like you use for a machine.'

She shows him the toolbox in the garage. He selects a spanner and a pair of pliers and spends an hour working on the piano. Then he sits down and plays a simple piece, made quaint by the click of the missing hammer.

'I am sorry we don't have anything better to offer you,' she says.

'You remember Orfeo? Orfeo did not have a piano, just a harp, very primitive, but the animals came and listened to him, the lion, the tiger, the horse, the cow, all of them. Congress of peace.'

Orfeo. So now he is Orfeo.

24. They drive down to the port and have coffee on a terrace above the harbour. She asks him about his time in Valldemossa. 'Did you find the audiences there receptive? I mean, did they appreciate your playing?'

'I played in the old monastery. The acoustics are not good. But the audience—yes, in the audience there were serious people, some of them.'

'Is that what you like—serious people? Do I count as a serious person?'

He looks her up and down. 'In Polish we talk of a person who is heavy, a person who is not made of air. You are a heavy person.'

She laughs. 'In English they say *solid—a solid person* or *a person of substance*. *Heavy* is reserved for fat people. I am glad to hear you don't think I am made of air, but you are wrong, I am not solid, not a person of substance.'

She thinks: *If you now say I am liquid, then I will begin to believe in you.* But he does not.

I am liquid. If you tried to hold me, I would flow out of your hands like water.

'You, on the other hand,' she says, 'are solid. Perhaps too solid for Chopin. Has anyone ever told you that?'

'Many people think Chopin is made of air,' he says. 'I try to correct them.'

'There is plenty of air in Chopin. And even more water. Running water. Liquid music. Debussy too.'

He inclines his head. Yes? No? She does not know how to interpret his gestures. Perhaps she never will. A foreigner.

'That is how I see it,' she says. 'But what do I know? In music I am just an amateur.'

25. He spends the afternoon in the back room improvising at the piano. Since she hears no clicking noises, she presumes that he is managing to skirt the dead key. Not lacking in ingenuity.

While he is occupied she ventures into the cottage that is now his territory. The bathroom bears a faint smell of eau de Cologne. Abstractedly she examines his travelling kit, neatly laid out on the shelf beneath the mirror. A razor. A hairbrush with an ebony handle. Pomade. Shampoo. An array of pillboxes, each with a label in Polish. A man from another era. Or perhaps all of Poland is like this: stuck in the past. Why is she so incurious about Poland?

26. She asks him to play for her. 'Play those little pieces by Lutosławski that you played in Barcelona.'

He plays the first three, with a click for the missing F.

'That is enough?'

'Yes, that is enough. I just wanted a change from Chopin.'

27. 'After Mallorca, where do you go?' she asks him.

'I have engagements in Russia. One in Saint Petersburg, one in Moscow.'

'Are you famous in Russia? Excuse my ignorance. I mean, do the Russians regard you highly?'

'No one regards me highly, nowhere in the world.

It's okay. I am the old generation. I am history. I should be in a museum, in a glass cabinet. But here I am. I am still alive. *It is a miracle*, I say to them. *If you don't believe, you can touch me.*'

She is confused. Who does not believe? Who is being invited to touch him? The Russians?

'You ought to be proud of yourself,' she says. 'Not everyone enters history. There are people who spend their whole lives trying to be part of history and fail. I will never be part of history, for example.'

'But you do not try,' he says.

'No, I don't try. I am content to be who I am.'

What she does not say is: *Why should I want to end up in history? What is history to me?*

28. 'Is there a coiffeur in this town?' he asks.

'Several. What do you need done? If all you need is a haircut, I can do it for you. I cut my sons' hair for years. I am perfectly competent.'

It is, to a degree, a test. How vain is he about that leonine head of hair?

Not vain at all, as it turns out. 'For you to cut my hair—it would be the greatest gift,' he says.

She seats him on the porch with a sheet around

his neck. He declines a mirror: his faith in her seems absolute. Through the operation he sits without opening his eyes, a dreamy smile on his lips. Is the touch of her fingers on his scalp all that it takes to satisfy him? Caressing someone's head: an unexpectedly intimate act.

'Your hair is very fine,' she says. 'More like a woman's than a man's.' What she does not say is that he is beginning to grow bald at the crown. But perhaps he knows.

Her father had a nurse to look after him in his last weeks and months. However, it was often she, Beatriz, who was called in to help. It was not a role she had been prepared for, yet she performed it quite adequately, to her own surprise. If the Pole were to fall ill now, she would look after him. She would find that perfectly natural. What is unnatural is that he arrives at her door not as an old man in need of care but as a would-be lover.

29. 'You have never told me about your marriage,' she says. 'Was it a happy marriage?'

'My marriage is long ago in the past. And in communist Poland too. Nineteen seventy-eight it was over. Nineteen seventy-eight is almost history.'

'Just because your marriage is history does not mean it was not real. Memories are real—you said so yourself. You must have memories.'

The Pole gives one of his little inward smiles. 'Some of us remember good memories. Some of us remember bad memories. We choose which memories we remember. Some memories, we put them in the underground. That is how you say it: the underground?'

'Yes, that is how they say it. The underground. The cemetery of bad memories. Tell me some of your good memories. What was your wife like? What was her name?'

'Her name was Małgorzata but everyone called her Gosia. She was a teacher. She taught English and German languages. From her I perfected my English.'

'Do you have a photograph of her?'

'No.'

Of course not. Why would he?

He does not ask about her own marriage and its associated memories, good and bad. He does not ask whether she carries a photograph of her husband wherever she goes. He does not ask about anything. Truly incurious.

30. That is one of the more intimate conversations they have. For the rest, when they are together, they are silent. She is not normally silent—with friends she can be exuberant, chatty—but from the Pole there seems to emanate a freeze on all frivolity. She tells herself it is a matter of the language—that if she were Polish or he were Spanish they would talk more easily, like any normal couple. But if he were Spanish he would be a different man, just as if she were Polish she would be a different woman. They are what they are: grown-ups, civilized people.

31. She takes him out to lunch in Fornalutx—not to the intimate little restaurant that she and her husband frequent but to one attached to a hotel that a century ago was the residence of a local eminence. At its centre is a courtyard open to the skies: birds swoop in and strut around among the tables or dip themselves in the fountain. No one is curious about the two of them, no one shows any interest. They are free beings, answerable to none.

She visits the ladies' room. Emerging from the shadows, she pauses in the doorway, waiting for him to catch sight of her, then threads her way towards him through the tables. His eyes are fixed on her, as are the eyes of the two waiters.

She is aware of the effect she can have on men. Grace: not such an antique concept after all. In Poland or Russia, she thinks, he will relive this moment, the moment when, crossing the floor towards him, came a vision of grace embodied. *What have we done to deserve this*, he will think, *guests, cooks, waiters, all of us? Grace that descends from the skies, shedding its radiance on us.*

32. It is their third day together in the house. Loreto has done her chores and gone home. She, Beatriz, tries to read but is too distracted. Time moves sluggishly. She wills it to pass.

Dusk falls. She taps at the cottage door. 'Witold? I have made us something to eat.'

They eat in silence. Afterwards she says: 'I am going to clear up, then I am going to retire. I will leave the back door unlocked. If you feel lonely during the night and want to visit, do so.'

That is all she says. She does not want a discussion.

She brushes her teeth, washes her face, combs her hair, inspects herself in the bathroom mirror. Looking at oneself in a mirror is something that women do in books and films, but she is not in a book or a film and she is not looking at herself. No, it is the being on the other side of the glass who is looking at her, to whose inspection she is submitting herself. What does that other see?

With an intense effort she tries to send herself through the glass, to inhabit that alien self, that alien gaze. No use.

She puts on her black nightdress, parts the curtains, switches off the light. Moonlight pours in. She is still a good-looking woman: there is that to hold onto. *Amazing, the way you have kept your looks!* says Margarita. *Two children and you still have the figure of an eighteen-year-old!* Well, let him marvel at his luck. But what would the two children in question say if they could see her now? *Mama, how could you!*

She hears the back door open, hears his footsteps, hears him enter the bedroom. Without a word he undresses; she averts her eyes. She feels his body stretch out beside hers, feels the barrel chest against her and the hair that covers it in a thick mat. *Like a bear!* she thinks. *What am I letting myself in for? Too late: no going back now.*

She helps him as best she can with the lovemaking. Though she has no experience of old men, she can guess what their troubles in bed will be, their deficiencies. It is a strange experience, and not a little frightening, to have that huge weight pressing down on her, but before long it is over.

'So now you have had me,' she says. 'You have had your gracious lady. Are you at last content?'

'My heart is full,' he says. He presses her hand to his chest. Dimly she can feel the beating of a heart, *trip-trip-trip*, faster than her own steady heart—in fact alarmingly fast. The last thing she wants is a corpse in her bed.

'I don't know what a full heart feels like,' she says, 'as opposed to an empty heart. But you must be careful. Do you hear me? Do you understand?'

'I hear you, *cariño*.'

Cariño. Where on earth did he pick that up?

33. She is not going to spend the night with this huge lump of a man in her bed. 'I must sleep now,' she says, 'and you must go. I will see you in the morning. Goodnight, Witold. Sleep well.'

She watches his shadowy outline as he puts on his clothes. A gleam of light as he opens the door, then he is gone.

Three more nights in Sóller. Is he going to expect her to accommodate him on each of them? A wave of tiredness sweeps over her. She wishes she were back in Barcelona in her own bed, in her own life, without these complications. She wishes, above all, to sleep.

34. She takes particular care, in the morning, with her clothes, with her makeup. By the time she appears in the kitchen the Pole has finished his breakfast. She offers her cheek to be kissed.

'Did you sleep well?' she asks. He nods.

Over her bowl of fruit she inspects him. How does he seem? Confused, mainly. Probably sleepless too.

You have only yourself to blame, she chides herself. Two strangers thrown together in the dark, performing an act neither was ready for. Actors. Performers. *You thought you would get away scot-free, you thought there would be no consequences, but you were wrong, wrong, wrong.*

'How about we go for a swim?' she offers. 'Have you brought a swimsuit? No? We can buy you one in Sóller if you like.'

They visit an outfitter's. Yellow is the only colour they have in the Pole's size.

It is still early. At her favourite beach the family groups have not yet arrived. The only people there are the serious swimmers.

It is a strange experience for the two of them, who mere hours ago were naked in bed together, to behold each other semi-naked in the glare of sunlight. What does she see? How thin, even spindly, his legs are. She hopes he will not notice the tracery of blue veins on her inner thighs.

You give me peace. Body wrestling against sweaty body. As much of a shock for the man as for the woman. After a duel like that, no room left for adoration, for veneration. Adoration sent packing.

In the water they part company. He stays in the shallows, she heads straight out into the deep.

Alone in the sea: a profound relief. She could dive down, metamorphose into a dolphin, feel the whole mess she has created wash away. What a stupid idea to invite a strange man to her husband's childhood home!

35. They are back at the house. 'I want to speak to you about Loreto,' she says. 'Loreto is a woman, she has a woman's eye. There is no point in trying to conceal from her what is going on. Nevertheless, we cannot be

flagrant. Do you understand what I am saying? We cannot insult her by carrying on an adultery—because that is what it is, that is its name—under her nose. She has her pride. She will walk out and not come back. And I will be humiliated.'

'I understand,' says the Pole. 'We do not behave like lovers.'

'Correct. We do not behave like lovers.'

'I have been your lover since the day I met you and no one knows. No one in the world can guard a secret better than I can.'

'If you really believe that then you are a fool. To me you are transparent. To Loreto you are transparent. To any woman you are transparent. What I am asking you to do has nothing to do with guarding secrets. I am asking you to maintain a fiction. Can you do that, in a respectful way?'

The Pole bows his head. 'Dante the poet was the lover of Beatrice and no one knew.'

'That is nonsense. Beatrice knew. All her friends knew. They giggled about it, like all girls do. Do you really think you are Dante, Witold?'

'No, I am not Dante. I am not inspired. And I am not clever with words.'

36. In the afternoon they go for a walk, following the same route up the hillside.

'Tell me more about your daughter,' she says. 'Does she take after you or after her mother?'

'If she looks like me it would be a disaster. No, she looks like her mother.'

'And her inner life? Does she follow her mother in her passions or does she follow you?'

'Yes? No? I cannot say. A daughter does not show to her father her passions.'

She lets it pass. *Passion*: what does he think the word means? Naked bodies on a summer night?

All their conversations seem to be like that: coins passed back and forth in the dark, in ignorance of what they are worth.

Sometimes she has the feeling that he is not listening to what she says, only to the tone of her voice, as if she were singing rather than speaking. She is not fond of her own voice—too low, too soft—but he seems to drink it in. Always he sees the best in her.

Something unnatural in loving without expecting to be loved in return.

Why is she with him? Why has she brought him here? What if anything does she find pleasing about him? There is an answer: that he so transparently takes pleasure in her. When she walks into the room, his face, usually so dour, lights up. In the gaze that bathes her there is a quantum of male desire, but finally it is a gaze of admiration, of dazzlement, as though he cannot believe his luck. It pleases her to offer herself to his gaze.

She has come to like his hands too. It amuses her to think that he makes his living by manual labour.

There are other features, however, that irritate her: his stiffness, his remoteness from the world around him, above all the pompous way he talks. Everything he says, everything he does has a formal feel to it. Even in her arms he does not seem able to relax. A comical spectacle, the two of them, making their love in English, a tongue whose erotic reaches are closed to them.

Is she too hard on him? Does she lack tenderness? Is each of us born with a certain quota of tenderness, and did she expend all her tenderness on her husband and children, leaving nothing for this late lover?

If she does not love him, what is the name of the feeling she has for him, the feeling that has led her down this questionable path?

If she had to pin it down, she would call it pity. He fell in love with her and she took pity on him and out of pity gave him his desire. That was how it happened; that was her mistake.

38. Her husband telephones. 'How are you getting on with your musician friend?' he asks.

'Not too badly. He came in yesterday by bus from Valldemossa. He has fixed up the piano in the back room, as far as it can be fixed, which will be useful for us. I'll take him for a drive this afternoon and show him some of the island. He leaves tomorrow.'

'And at a personal level?'

'At a personal level? He and I get along perfectly well. He is a bit *arisco*, a bit dour, but I don't mind that.'

She is unused to lying, but on the telephone it is not so difficult. And they do not count as great lies. In the end they will amount to nothing. Whatever occurred here in Sóller will be swept into the past and forgotten.

38. On each of the three nights left to them the Pole visits her in her bed. She is reminded of the story of the Greek girl who, nervous that the dark stranger in her bed might turn out to be a monster, lit a lamp and discovered he was a god. Well, she, Beatriz, needs no

lamp. The stranger in her bed may not be a monster but he is certainly no god.

Why did the girl need to see her visitor anyway? Was the weight, the crushing pressure of an alien male body, not enough?

The shock of the new. A bright shock, like being electrocuted, not a dark one, like being swept away and buried in a mudslide.

There is a moment on the second night when out of the past there re-emerges the delicious feeling of falling. She had thought it gone forever, that it belonged only to youth or even to childhood: the terror and delight of shooting down a water slide, when the will is abdicated and one is, briefly, pure experience.

What else does she remember? Fingers playing on her skin, drawing music out of her. A musician's touch.

Sometimes, while he is about his erotic business, her mind drifts idly to the shopping she must ask Loreto to do, to the appointment she has missed with the dentist.

As a lover the man is capable but not quite capable enough. No matter how resolute the spirit, he cannot prevent the creakiness of his physical being, his lack of vital force, from infecting his lovemaking. He covers up for it as best he can, and, each time he takes his departure from her bed, thanks her: 'I thank you from my heart.' Her own heart goes out to him at those moments, in pity if not in love. So hard to be a man!

She cannot bring herself to caress him. He is aware, she knows, of this reluctance on her part, this physical distaste. Awareness of it enters into his ritual thanks. *Thank you for descending so far*.

She ought to feel guilty. One should not go to bed with a man whom one does not desire. But she feels no guilt. *I give enough*, she says to herself. *And it is not forever*.

39. *Be-a-triz*, he whispers into her ear. *I will die with your name on my lips*.

40. She is in his arms. It is their last night together. She speaks. 'This is not easy to say, Witold, but tonight we have come to the end. We are not going to see each other again. It makes life too difficult for me. I do not need to explain. Just accept it.'

She is glad they are in the dark. She does not like hurting people; she does not want to see a stricken look of any kind on his face.

'Don't think badly of me. Please. There is a bus to

Valldemossa at eight-fifteen. I will drive you to the bus station.'

She has rehearsed her speech beforehand, therefore it is understandable that the moment should feel artificial, as though she were standing somewhere outside, or hovering overhead, hearing the woman's voice, watching for the man's reaction.

The man reacts by slackening his embrace, which a moment ago was warm but has now turned cold; he reacts by turning away from her, getting up, reaching for his clothes. He reacts by finding his way to the door (with a slight stumble in the dark) and making his exit; if she listens hard she can hear the click as the kitchen door closes behind him.

She allows herself to exhale. She is glad, unutterably glad, that he did not react with anger, with hurt pride, that he did not humiliate himself by pleading. If he had pleaded she would have turned against him forever.

41. He does make a plea, after all, one last plea, on the way to the bus the next morning. 'After Russia is finished we can fly to Brazil,' he says. 'You can swim in the sea in Brazil.'

'No,' she says. 'I am not going to follow you around the world—you or any other man. No.'

They arrive at the bus stop. 'I am not going to wait,' she says. 'Goodbye.' She kisses him on the lips. Then she is gone.

42. Back home she checks the cottage. He has left no trace behind, no physical trace. A good guest.

43. *'El señor vuelve?'* asks Loreto.

'No, el señor ha sido llamado de vuelta a su tierra natal. A Polonia. No volverá.' The gentleman will not be coming back.

44. For the rest of the day she goes about her routines slowly, calmly, deliberately. She is still in a state of shock, she recognizes, and has been so ever since the Pole first manifested himself in her bedroom. If she can stay calm and allow time to do its work, the state of shock—which she pictures as a sheet wound around her so tightly that she can barely breathe—will lose its grip and life will resume its accustomed orderliness.

A sheet or else a frame, like the one in the Greek story, a bed in which one's limbs are crushed until one fits someone else's idea of how one should be.

The Pole too, for all she knows. The Pole, with his

inconveniently long legs and big hands, may have been crushed and contorted in a frame of his own.

45. In the days before she flies back to Barcelona she has time to reorder her memories and settle on the story she is going to tell herself, the story that will become her story. She *had a fling*, she decides (she uses the English term). She had a fling with a visiting musician, which had its rewards but is now over. If Margarita, who is intuitive, taxes her with it (*You have been with someone! I can see it!*), she will not dissemble. *It was that Polish pianist you brought to Barcelona—you remember him? He was playing at the Chopin festival. He was free, I was free, we spent a few days together. Nothing serious. I am sure he has lots of affairs.*

She is prepared to entertain the possibility that her story may be incomplete and even in certain respects untrue. But, looking into her heart, she can find no dark residue: no regret, no sorrow, no longings—nothing to trouble the future.

Nothing serious. Is love a state of mind, a state of being, a phenomenon, a fashion that recedes, even as we watch it, into the past, into the backward reaches of history? The Pole was in love with her, *seriously* in love—and probably still is—but the Pole himself is a relic of history, of an age when desire had to be infused with a tincture of the unattainable before it could pass as the real thing. What of her, Beatriz, his beloved? Well, she was certainly not unattainable. On the contrary, she was all too attainable. *Come and visit me in my house. Come and visit me in my bed.* If she has saved herself, in the end, from the stigma of the too easily attainable, it was only by sending the Pole packing—the Pole who is no doubt at this very moment working up a story of his own about a cruel Spanish mistress who left a scar on his heart that will take a long time to heal.

FOUR

1. For a while after her return to Barcelona she continues in a state of mild shock. It surprises her that what occurred in Mallorca can have an effect so long-lasting, like a bomb that explodes harmlessly but leaves one deafened.

Being in a state of shock does not prevent her from plunging back into activity. She has been drafted onto a committee to fund residencies for rising young musicians: she spends hours every day on the telephone. And then there is the Concert Circle, whose audiences are dwindling as regulars grow old or infirm. Tomás Lesinski has died; his wife Ester is in the process of moving to France to live with their daughter. The grant that the Circle receives from the city is about to be slashed by half ('financial stringencies'): they will have to trim their programme from ten concerts a year to six.

She does not miss the Pole, not at all. He writes to her. She deletes his letters without reading them.

2. In October of 2019, visiting the Sala Mompou, she is

told by a secretary that someone is trying to contact her from Germany. 'It is about a musician who once played here, I didn't catch the name, it sounded Russian. She left her number.'

She calls the number and hears a recorded message in German. Speaking English, she leaves her name.

Her call is returned. 'This is Ewa Reichert, my father is Witold Walczykiewicz, he passed away, perhaps you know this?'

'No, I did not know. I am sorry. Please accept my condolences.'

'He was ill for a long time.'

'I knew nothing of this. I am afraid I lost touch with your father some time ago. He will be remembered. He was a great pianist.'

'Yes. There are some things for you that he left behind.'

'Oh? What kind of things?'

'I have not seen. They are still in Warsaw, in the apartment. You were there?'

'I have never been to Warsaw, Mrs Reichert, Ewa. I have never been to Poland. Are you sure you have the right person?'

'This is the number that I called, and now you call me, so it is you—no?'

'I understand. Can you send these items to me?'

'I am in Berlin, I cannot send anything. I give you the name of the neighbour in Warsaw, then you can make arrangements. Her name is Pani Jablońska, for a long time she was a friend of my father. All the items for you she has put in a box with your name. Only you must act soon. I wait only for the documents from the lawyer, then I sell the apartment. Or perhaps it is not important to you, I don't know, it is your decision. But I say again, you must please act soon. There is a *wohltätige Organisation* in Warsaw, I don't know how you say it in English: I arrange that they come and take away everything in the apartment, make it clean, that is how they work. So if you want these things, you call Pani Jablońska.'

She dictates an address and telephone number in Warsaw.

'Thank you. I will speak to Pani Jablońska and see what can be done. You have no idea what these things are that your father wanted me to have?'

'No. My father did never tell me his secrets. Also, Pani Jablońska will not speak English, so you must have translation when you telephone.'

'Thank you. Thank you for letting me know. Goodbye.'

Secrets. So she is one of the Pole's secrets: the Barcelona secret. What other secrets did he leave behind in cities around the world?

3. She calls a courier company. Yes, they operate in Poland, they operate everywhere in Europe. Yes, they can pick up a consignment from an address in Warsaw. What does the consignment consist of? A box? A large box? A small box? For an item of under five kilograms, for door-to-door pick-up and delivery, the charge will be one hundred and eighty Euros, plus customs duties if there are customs duties, depending on what is in the box. What is in the box? Photographs? CDs? Used CDs? Normally there no customs duties on such items within the EU. Shall they go ahead?

First let me make arrangements for the pick-up, she says. I will call you back.

4. One of the violinists in the chamber orchestra that uses the Sala Mompou is a Russian. She catches him after a rehearsal. 'Can you spare me a minute? I need to get a message to a lady in Poland. I have her number here. If I call her, can you speak to her and give her a message—that a courier will be coming on Friday to fetch the box? Can you do that for me?'

'I don't speak Polish,' says the violinist. 'Polish is not Russian, is different language.'

'Yes, I know, but this is an elderly lady, she has lived through a lot of history, she must know some Russian, and it is a very simple message.'

'Speak Russian to Poles is like insult, but for you I try. Courier is coming Friday?'

'Courier is coming Friday, she must give him the box.' She taps in Pani Jabłońska's number and hands over the phone.

There is no reply.

'Write the text in Russian and I will send it. The text is: *Good day, Pani Jabłońska. My name is Beatriz, I am the friend of Pan Witold. A courier will come on Friday. Please give the box to the courier.*'

'I write in Roman alphabet,' says the violinist. He writes: *Dobri den, Pani Jabłońska. Menya zovut Beatriz, ya drug...* You write his name. *Kuryer priyedet v pyatnitsu. Pazhaluysta, otdayte korobku kuryeru.* 'Is not good Russian, but maybe Polish lady understands. I go now. You tell me if you have success, yes?' And he hurries off.

There is no reply to the Russian's text. Early the next morning, with the Russian words at hand ready to be repeated, she telephones Pani Jabłońska. Again there is no reply. She calls at all hours, that day and that night, without result.

5. What can the Pole have left for her? Whatever it is, can it be worth all this fuss? Does she want to hear yet more of his recordings of Chopin?

The future lies open before her and the Pole is trying to draw her back. From the grave he stretches out a great claw to drag her into the past. Well, she does not have to submit. She can shrug off the claw. To the courier man she can say, *Cancel my order*. To the daughter she can say, *It is too much trouble, speaking Russian gibberish to Pani Jabłońska, who will not understand anyway. So go ahead, clear out your father's apartment, sell everything, be rid of it*. To the man in the grave she can say, *You have no power over me. You are dead. Being dead may be a new experience for you but you will get used to it. It is a not uncommon fate to find oneself dead and forgotten*.

6. She telephones the daughter again, Ewa. 'I have been in touch with a courier company. They say they can fetch the box, no problem. The problem is Pani Jabłońska. She does not answer my calls. Perhaps

something has happened to her—I don't know. Is there anyone else who can give the box to the courier?'

'There is the *Agentur*, they are selling the apartment, they have keys. You can call the *Agentur* and explain, yes?'

'Explain what, Ewa?' She cannot keep the sharpness from her voice.

There are noises in the background. '*Ich komme!*' cries Ewa. 'I must go now. I send you the number of the *Agentur*, then you can explain. Goodbye.'

Explain what?

7. The apartment is not at all what she had expected. To begin with, it is not in Warsaw proper but in the outer suburbs. From the street where the taxi drops her she has to cross a car park and a playground where three boys are racing their bicycles, with a little white dog scurrying after them, yapping and trying to bite their tyres. And then the apartment block itself is devoid of all character, built to the same drab plan as blocks in the working-class sections of Barcelona. Why would he choose to live here of all places?

Early for her appointment, she makes a circuit of the block. From an upstairs balcony an old woman in black peers at her suspiciously. It is October; the trees—maples?—are dropping their leaves.

In the entryway she meets the agent, a tall young man in an ill-fitting suit. He shakes her hand; his English, it turns out, is rudimentary.

'Thank you for coming,' she says. 'You understand, I do not want to buy the apartment, I have come only to fetch something. I need no more than a minute of your time.'

He makes no move. Has he understood?

'You open the door for me.' She makes a twisting motion: a key turning in a lock. 'I pick up the box. Then we go. You are a free man. That is all. Okay?'

'Okay,' he says.

There is a problem with the door. The key on his ring, the key that is labelled 2-30—he shows her the label, the number of the apartment—does not fit the keyhole. He shrugs helplessly? *What can I do?* his expression says.

She takes the keyring from him, tries another key. The door opens. 'See?' she says.

She enters, the agent following.

She had expected mahogany furniture, gloom, dust, creaking bookcases, spiders in the corners. In fact, save for a stack of cartons in a corner and four plastic chairs nested into one another, the front room is bare, and—because the curtains have been taken down—flooded with sunlight.

She peers into a minuscule kitchen, into a bathroom with a plastic shower curtain brown with age.

'You are sure this is the correct apartment?' she asks.

The agent shows her the key again, 2-30, the key that does not fit.

It occurs to her that the whole thing may be a trick, a malicious trick: not only not the correct apartment, but also not the correct apartment block, not the correct quarter of the city, perhaps not even the correct house agent. A trick for which only one person can be responsible: the daughter in Berlin, Ewa. Ewa has, out of ill will, sent her off on a pointless errand. *Who is she, this Beatriz? Just another of my father's many girlfriends.*

But she is wrong. No trick. The second room is positively cluttered. It contains a bed (single), two chests of drawers, a rack of men's clothes, an ironing table with a plastic sunflower in a vase, a mirror in an ornate gilt frame, a massive rolltop desk with a formidable typewriter.

There is a third room too, with another kitchen and another bathroom leading off it. This room is bare save for a piano. On one wall is a framed advertisement for a recital at Wigmore Hall, dated 1991, with an image of one of the Pole's younger selves staring abstractedly into the distance. On the piano lid: a picture of young Witold, black and white, unsmiling, receiving some kind of award from a man in a frockcoat; a plaster bust of Johann Sebastian Bach; a more recent picture of Witold, hands clasped, at the centre of a row of women in sparkling evening dress, among whom she recognizes, astonishingly, herself. The Concert Circle sisterhood as it was in 2015, minus Margarita! She has never seen the photograph before. Where did he lay his hands on it?

'See!' she says, pointing.

The house agent peers over her shoulder. 'It is you,' he says.

'Yes,' she says, 'it is me.' Indeed it is! Year after year, unbeknown to her, her image has been casting its faint light over this dreary quarter of this alien city.

But what of the box, the precious box that the elusive Pani Jablońska has prepared for her, the box for whose sake she has crossed half a continent?

The cartons in the front room—there must be twenty of them—have labels scrawled on them that she cannot make out. 'Can you help me?' she says to the young man. 'Can you tell me what these boxes contain?'

The young man takes off his jacket and springs into action. 'This...this...this—books. All books. Only this...this—no books.' He extracts two boxes from the pile. With a kitchen knife she opens them. Men's clothing, smelling of camphor; kitchenware; medicines; odds and ends; nothing for her.

'You look for this?' says the agent. He is holding out a small grey box with a label on it. She reads the label: WITOLD WALCZYKIEWICZ 19.VII.2019. She opens the box. It contains a porcelain urn and the urn contains ash.

'Where did you find it?' she asks.

The agent indicates a shelf in the kitchen.

'Put it back, please.'

She calls Ewa's number, leaves a message: 'Ewa, I am in your father's apartment. I have the house agent with me. We can't find Pani Jabłońska's box. Please call urgently.'

Idly the agent fingers a scale on the piano. He tries to sit down, but the piano stool resists. From its recess he extracts a cardboard box file. On the file is pasted a label with her name and the telephone number of the Sala Mompou.

She opens the file. Loose papers. A binder. A photograph of her, wearing a swimsuit and a wide straw hat, taken years ago, that he must have stolen from the house in Sóller.

'This is it,' she says. 'This is what we have been looking for. Thank you, thank you. I am most grateful. You are free to go now. I will stay behind briefly. I will lock the door behind me when I leave. Is that okay?'

The young man seems dubious. Does he not trust her? She holds out a hand, which after a moment's hesitation he takes. 'Thank you again. Goodbye. *Do widzenia*.' And she watches him leave.

8. She examines the papers: printouts of the handful of emails that passed between the two of them, nothing more. She opens the binder. It contains what are evidently poems, in Polish, one to a page, typewritten and numbered I—LXXXIV.

So this is what Witold W, the less and less famous pianist, has left for her: not music but some kind of manuscript. And this is where he must have been living when he prepared it: in this dreary little apartment in this featureless quarter of the city of his birth. Puzzling. But perhaps this was his notion of a monk's cell, his place of retreat from the world.

She pages through the poems, searching for her name amid the snarl of consonants, and finds it several times—not Beatriz but Beatrice. Thus: a book of Beatrice, put together by an obscure follower of Dante.

9. She could put all this stuff back in the recess of the piano stool and leave it to be carted away to the auction house. Or she could add it to the box of miscellaneous rubbish in the front room, to end its life amid food wrappers and orange rinds and styrofoam in a dump somewhere in the wasteland of the Polish countryside. She could do that and draw the door closed behind her (*click!*) and call a taxi and get to the airport in time for her late-afternoon flight to Barcelona via Frankfurt and never give another thought to the Pole and his book of Beatrice.

Alternatively, she could take the poems back to Barcelona and get someone to translate them and have them hand-printed on rag paper in a limited edition of ten copies, *El libro de Beatriz* de W.W. One copy for the daughter in Berlin, to prove that she, Beatriz/Beatrice, was no whore, the rest to be stored away in a cupboard for her sons to discover after her death and learn what heights, what depths of passion their mother could inspire, even in her mature years.

What to do? Take the poems with her or leave them here, abandon them, forget about them? The man is dead. The daughter doesn't care. There is no one to answer to but herself.

10. She must read Dante. Her education never took her that far. She knows the picture of him, the famous picture, but not the poetry. Features not unlike the Pole's. The same scowl.

You should smile more, she told him once. *You have a nice smile. People would warm to you if you could learn to smile.*

11. She too is warming to the Pole, now that she has his testament in her hands. It so happens that she does not go in for grand, hopeless passions—not part of her constitution, evidently—but that does not mean she does not admire grand passions in others. It is pleasing to know that he did not forget her, that far from forgetting her he celebrated her in verse. His Beatrice. It could not have been easy. Even in Spanish getting words to rhyme takes skill. Think of doing it in Polish!

12. She should have a talk with the daughter. On the

telephone the daughter came across as cold and inconsiderate, but maybe that was just the ghost of the German language haunting her English. She could drop in on her in her busy-busy restaurant in Berlin. Hello, Ewa, let me introduce myself. I am Beatriz, the lady friend of your father's from Barcelona. If you have the time, if you are not needed in the kitchen, can we sit down and have a chat? You probably think I am one of those harpies who sink their claws into famous men and suck the blood out of them. Well, you are wrong. I am not like that at all. I did not seek your father's attention. It was he who fell in love with me. I could have slammed the door in his face, but I didn't. I treated him gently, as gently as I could. The memories I left him with were, for the most part, happy. If you do not believe me, take a look: here are the poems he wrote for me.

13. The clock is ticking. It is three in the afternoon. If she wants to sleep in her own bed tonight she must move. Alternatively, she could spend the night in Warsaw, fly out in the morning. She could make herself at home in this apartment, explore the neighbourhood, get a meal somewhere, authentic Polish food (what might that be? blood sausage, boiled potatoes, sauerkraut?), sleep in

the dead man's bed. There are practical problems (no electricity, no bedclothes), but they are not insuperable. If the man suffered for her—indeed, pined for her—does she not owe it to him to suffer a little in return?

14. She leaves a message on her husband's phone: *Staying on in Warsaw. Back tomorrow.*

15. The boys with their bicycles have gone, along with the dog. She makes a tour of the neighbourhood. There is nothing worth seeing, nothing she could not find back home. From a poky little shop (*Supermarket* says the sign) she buys a packet of dried apricots, a packet of biscuits, a bottle of water. She returns to the apartment and, using the last of the daylight, extracts a woollen sweater and a pair of corduroy trousers from the boxes. Her nightwear. The water supply is not cut off, she is able to wash.

16. She sleeps, does not dream. She never dreams. However, during the night she wakes briefly, sensing someone else in the apartment. 'Witold, if that is you, come and lie with me,' she murmurs into the darkness. There is no answering movement, no sound. She goes back to sleep.

17. In the morning she calls for a taxi and by 9 a.m. is at the airport. She has a long wait for her flight; she uses it to have a leisurely breakfast, a massage, a manicure. By 6 p.m. she is home, rested and smiling.

'I got your message,' says her husband. 'How was the trip? Do I need to feel jealous?'

'The man is dead,' she says. 'How can you feel jealous?'

'Alienation of affections,' he says. 'Hasn't he alienated your affections?'

'Don't be ridiculous. I was never in love with him. He was in love with me. A one-sided affair. That's all.'

'And you brought back the box, the famous box? What was in it?'

'There was a misunderstanding. I misunderstood the daughter. I was expecting something personal, but all he left was a book he had published on Chopin, in Polish. As a keepsake. A memento.'

'So it was a waste of time, the whole trip.'

'Not entirely. I got to see Poland, or some of it. I got to see where Witold lived. I got to say goodbye.'

'He was important to you, wasn't he.'

'No, not important, not in himself. But one needs to

be reassured every now and again, if one is a woman. One needs proof that one can still make an impression.'

'And I do not provide that proof?'

'Yes, you do. But not enough.'

18. *Not important.* Is she lying? *I was never in love with him.* True. *He was in love with me.* True. Where is the lie in that?

She has secrets from her husband, as he has secrets from her. In a good marriage the partners respect each other's right to have secrets. She has a good marriage; and what passed in Mallorca counts as one of her secrets.

Her husband is a man of the world. He knows how broad a field *We were not lovers* can cover: what it can include, what it excludes. It excludes *My heart belongs to him*. Her heart has never belonged to the Pole.

19. The book about Chopin, the keepsake, is not a fiction. She took it from one of the boxes in the apartment, brought it back so that she could say to her husband, *See: his last gift to me.*

FIVE

1. She calls up a translation program, Polish to Spanish, and types in the first poem of the eighty-four, taking pains to include every single dot and stroke and curlicue. What comes out after she presses the button makes little sense. There are three men in the poem: Homer, Dante Alighieri, and an unnamed vagabond who, with an animal—presumably a dog—at his side, follows in their footsteps, haunting crowded cities and asking people for money. This beggar meets a woman with a beautiful pink birthmark, who brings him peace. After which he finds himself in Warsaw, city of his birth and death, singing praises of the poet—Homer? Dante?—who showed him the way.

The beggar is clearly the Pole himself, while she, Beatriz, is presumably the woman with the birthmark. But why a birthmark? She has no birthmark. Is the birthmark a symbol of some kind? A symbol of a hidden flaw, perhaps, concealed by her clothing?

She does not demand that the computer provide a perfect translation. All she wants is an answer to the question: Is the tone of the poems positive or negative, celebratory or accusatory? Are they a hymn to the beloved; or on the contrary are they a bitter parting shot from a rejected lover? A simple enough question; but the computer is as tone-deaf as it is stupid.

2. Tomás, her elder son, the one who has always been closer to her, comes to lunch with his wife and child. After lunch she has a chance to speak to him alone. 'You don't happen to know anyone who speaks Polish, do you? I need some translation done.'

'Polish? No, I don't. What exactly do you need translated?'

'It's a long story, Tomás. There was a Polish man, quite a while ago, who was keen on me. He died recently, and his daughter found a suite of poems that he had written, apparently addressed to me, which she has passed on. I'm sure they are not great poetry, but it's sad to think he devoted so much labour to them and no one is ever going to read them. I have tried the computer, but the language is too complicated for it.'

'I'll ask around. I know someone at the university in Vic. They have a unit there that specializes in language teaching. Maybe there is a Polish specialist on the staff.

I'll find out. Was he in love with you, this Pole? Who was he?'

'He was a pianist, quite well known. He recorded for DGG. We met when he came to play for the Circle. He had rather unrealistic ideas about me. He wanted me to run away with him to Brazil.'

'He wanted you to give up everything, just like that, and go off with him?'

'Well, he was smitten. I didn't take him seriously. But now there are these poems. I feel a bit guilty. I feel I have a duty to read them. See what you can find. But please don't tell your father. It will only complicate matters.'

3. The next day Tomás calls. Unfortunately they don't teach Polish at Vic. The people there suggest she try the Polish consulate.

On the website of the Polish consulate she finds a brief list of accredited translators. She calls the first on the list: Clara Weisz Urizza, BA (Trieste), Dip.Tr. (Milan). 'I have a text in Polish that I want translated. Can you tell me what you charge?'

'It depends on what kind of text. Is it a legal document?'

'It is a set of poems, eighty-four in total, most of them quite short.'

'Poetry? I am not a literary translator. Normally I translate commercial and legal documents. But send me a sample and I will see what I can do.'

'I would prefer to bring the poems in person. I don't want them to circulate.'

'I have a day job at a travel agency.' She names a travel agency on Las Ramblas. 'You can drop a sample off there.'

'I would prefer to deal with you face to face. If that is not possible, say so, and I will make other arrangements.'

4. On Sunday she takes a taxi to Señora Weisz's address in Gracia. Señora Weisz turns out to be a grey-haired woman with an overflowing bust who speaks rapid Castilian with an Italian accent. The apartment is overheated, nevertheless she wears a sweater.

She offers coffee and too-sweet pastries. 'I confess I have never tried to translate poetry before,' she says. 'I hope it is not too modern.'

She, Beatriz, hands over copies she has made of the first ten poems. 'The author was an acquaintance from

Warsaw. He is deceased now. He was not a professional writer. I have no idea of the quality of the verse.'

'What is your desire?' says Señora Weisz. 'Do you want translations that you can publish?'

'No, not at all. We—that is to say, his daughter and I—have no plans for publication. As a first step I would like to get some idea of what the poems say, what they are about.'

Señora Weisz pages through the poems, shaking her head. 'These poems—I can translate the words for you, I can turn Polish words into Spanish words, but I cannot say, "This is what the poem is about, this is what it means." Do you understand what I am saying? Normally I translate legal documents, contracts. When I translate a contract I must be prepared to swear that the translation is correct. That is what is required from an accredited translator. But interpreting the contract, saying what it means, that is not my job—that is a job for a lawyer. Do I make myself clear? So: I translate your poems for you, and then you decide what they mean.'

'Very well. What will you charge?'

'The charge is seventy-five Euros per hour, that is the standard rate, we are all the same. How many hours? Eighty poems, you say, one page per poem. Maybe ten hours, maybe twenty, maybe more, I cannot say. For me poetry is a new field.'

'Some of the poems are longer than a page, so the page count may be more like a hundred. Can you translate the first poem for me now? Just a rough translation. So that I can get an idea of the tone. I will pay you for the hour.'

'The first poem. It says: The stranger must know that this man has travelled for many years and played the harp in many cities and spoken to animals. The stranger must know that this man—he does not tell the man's name—followed the footsteps of Homer and Dante and stayed in dark forests and crossed the wine-coloured sea. Then the poem says this: He found the perfect rose between the legs of a certain woman, and thus attained final peace. He sings his song in Warsaw, the city where he was born and died, and he sings it in praise of the woman who showed him the way.'

Between the legs of a woman. Nothing about a birthmark. Nothing about a dog. 'That is the end?'

'That is the end.'

'Can you do the second poem too?'

'There is an epigraph: *Per entro i mie' disiri, che ti manavano ad amar lo bene*. The love you felt for me led you to love of the good. That's Dante in old Italian. The poem says this: When he was a dandy, a young man of fashion—you understand?—he liked to look at a particular woman but he could not have her, could not possess her. Her throat is bare, she swings her skirt, something like that. So all the desire, the male desire, climbs up from his private parts, climbs through his blood and his—I would have to look up the correct word in Spanish, it is a medical term—into his eyes. He stares with his eyes and through his eyes he possesses her. Then he goes to a public meeting and he chooses a pretty girl and employs her as a *biombo* or a *pantalla*, it is not clear, some kind of curtain or screen, while with his eyes he eats up the far one, the far woman, whose name is Beatrice, *la modesta* (he uses the Italian word or maybe Spanish, it is the same). Modesty, he says, is her highest virtue, also grace and goodness. Then he says: I had no luck, I came too late, I lived too far away, I had only her picture in my eyes, which is like a bird that flutters in memory. This poem is difficult, much more difficult than the first one, I would have to work on it.'

'Thank you. It is, as you say, a difficult poem. I too

don't understand it. Let me pay you, and let me go away and think about it—think whether I want the whole set translated.'

She counts out the fee in notes.

'He says Beatrice,' says Señora Weisz. 'That is not you. That is the girlfriend of the poet Dante.'

'Correct,' she says. 'The Beatrice in the poem has been dead for many years. Whereas I am still alive. Goodbye. I will let you know what I decide.'

Between Señora Weisz and herself there passes something like a smile of complicity.

5. *The love you felt for me led you to love of the good*. He should have written: *The love I felt for you led me to love of the good*. That would have made it clearer: having parted from his beloved, or been parted, he turned the ache of separation into a project of making himself a better man.

Dante and Beatrice: he was using the wrong myth. Misguided. She is no Beatrice, no saint.

What would have been the right myth? Orpheus and Eurydice? Beauty and the Beast?

6. She turns back to the first poem, the poem that

baffled the computer yet spoke so clearly to Señora Weisz. *Homera i Dantego Alighieri* are clearly Homer and Dante, and *idealną różę* must be *una rosa ideal*, an ideal rose. In that case, *wcześniej między nogami jego pani osiągając idealną różę* must be the bit about finding the rose, about attaining transcendence through sexual love; but finding it *between her legs*—what a vulgar way of putting it! No wonder Señora Weisz baulked when she brought out the words. *What am I letting myself in for?* she must have thought to herself. *And is there even worse to come?*

First Pani Jablońska, then the daughter in Berlin—Ewa—and now Señora Weisz. The circle is widening. When Pani Jablońska set aside the manuscript for the mystery woman in Spain, she must surely have sneaked a look at it and been struck by that glaring intimacy on the very first page. And Ewa, despite her denials, must have seen it too. No wonder she was so sniffy on the telephone! How humiliating! How galling!

7. She, Beatriz, comes from a cultivated family. Her grandfather, her father's father, had as a student at the University of Salamanca been witness to a public book-burning and had never forgotten it. *A true act*

of barbarity, he called it. In due course he became a professor of law and assembled a considerable library, which after his death went to his eldest son, her uncle Federico. *Burning books is a prelude to burning people*, her grandfather had said, an utterance that became part of the family's folklore. He passed away when she was five years old; she remembers him only as a stout old man with a prickly beard and a cane with an ivory handle.

Burning letters is not the same as burning books. People burn old letters every day of the week. They burn them because they contain nothing of abiding interest or because they have become an embarrassment: letters from childhood sweethearts, for example. The same holds true, more or less, for diaries. But the Pole's eighty-four poems are not letters except in a certain, unusual sense, nor do they constitute a diary, again except in a certain sense. They constitute a manuscript, that is to say, the embryo of a book. Burning the poems would be more like burning a book than burning old letters. The question is, would burning the poems be an act of barbarity, a prelude to burning people?

The answer is not wholly obvious. In Spain the Pole is a nobody, the record of his love affairs of no interest. Back in Poland, however, he is not a nobody. In Poland there may be a degree of interest, perhaps even a degree of pride, in what a noted interpreter of Poland's national composer has to say about the time he spent between the legs of women. Burning his poems may indeed, to Poles, constitute an act of barbarity. The civilized thing to do would be to return the poems to Poland, to the Chopin Museum or the National Patriotic Library, for their manuscript collection. To return them anonymously, eliminating all trace of herself, so that no one will ever come knocking at the door, now or in the future, saying, 'Are you the original of Beatrice? Are you the woman from Barcelona between whose legs Witold Walczykiewicz had his spiritual revelations?'

8. For days she mulls over the question: Should she burn the poems, or on the contrary should she commission Senõra Weisz to translate them (at no small cost); and, if the latter, is she prepared to read Señora Weisz's translations and thereby submit herself to probable pain and humiliation?

She mulls over the question; then, when the mulling has run its course, gives herself a shake and turns her attention to other things. The folder with the eighty-four poems goes into the bottom drawer of her desk.

Even in the bottom drawer, however, the poems refuse to be forgotten. They burn there with a slow fire.

The Pole wrote the poems to tell her that he went on loving her long after their time together in Mallorca. But he could have achieved the same with a simple letter in the mail: 'My dearest Beatriz, from my deathbed I write to tell you that I loved you to the end. Your faithful servant, Witold.' Therefore, why *poems*? And why so many of them?

The answer can only be: because he wanted not merely to *say* that he loved her but to prove it—prove it by performing for her sake a lengthy and inherently meaningless task. Nonetheless, why poems? If lengthy and meaningless labour is the criterion, why not engrave the Sermon on the Mount on a grain of rice and send it to her in a little plush box?

The answer: because, through his poems, he aspires to speak to her from beyond the grave. He wants to speak to her, to woo her, so that she will love him and keep him alive in her heart.

There are good kinds of love and bad kinds of love. What kind of love is it that burns day and night *between the legs of a woman* in the bottom drawer of her desk?

When she was young she would act on impulse.

She followed her impulses because she trusted them. Nowadays she is more prudent. The prudent course of action—no doubt about it—would be to distance herself from the fire, to wait until it had burnt itself out, then, perhaps, if she were still curious, to poke around in the ashes.

9. In Mallorca, in bed with her, he had called it her rose. At the time it felt false, a false word, and now, in his poems, it feels false too. Not a rose in truth, not a flower at all; but what?

She remembers her boys growing up, and their unending curiosity about girls. If girls did not have *it*, what did girls have? It could not be nothing; but if it was not nothing, what could it be? Curiosity; horror too. The two of them in the bath, splashing each other, laughing, raucous, overexcited. *What is it, mama! It: is that its name?*

It: where they came from, covered in blood and mucus, emerging into the noise and glare of the world. No wonder they wailed—*too much! too much!*—no wonder they clamoured to go back, to curl up in the old familiar nest and suck their thumbs and drowse in peace. And now the Pole, a big man—huge!—but no less babyish, emerging from her body and her bed no less confused, no less frightened. *It*: the rose that is no rose.

10. Boasting. That is how men defend themselves against the confusion. Her sons too, for all she knows, grown men now, men of the world. *I had her, that smart woman from Barcelona. I crushed her in my arms, I crumpled her rose.* The war between men and women, primeval, never-ending. *I had her, she was mine, read all about it.*

She hurt him. She wounded him in his pride. After that insult, all of his labour was self-protective, spinning nacre, layer upon layer of it, over the wound. She invited him into her bed, then she threw him out. His revenge on her: to freeze her, aestheticize her, turn her into an art-object, a Beatrice, a plaster saint to be venerated and carried in procession through the streets. *Mother of mercy.*

11. Yet if he wrote the poems to take revenge on her, how come the epigraph to poem 10, credited to Octavio Paz, whom he quotes in English? *A paradox of love: we love simultaneously a mortal body and an immortal soul.*

Without the attraction of the body, the lover could not love the soul. To the lover the desired body is a soul. Was that Witold's story too: that through loving her body he came to love her soul? Fair enough. But it does not answer the question: why *her* body, why *her* soul?

Go back to Beatrice, the real Beatrice. What was it that made Dante choose her over all other women? Or go back to Mary. What was it about Mary full of grace that made God decide to visit her by night? What flexion of the lip, what arch of the eyebrow, what contour of the buttock? At what moment did she, Beatriz, the woman whose job it was to take the visiting soloist out to dinner that fatal evening in 2015, become his destined one? What was it about *her* that brought about her election? Where was the divine in her, that evening? And where is the divine in her now?

12. Out of the blue, a call from Poland. *Vous parlez français, Madame?* Pani Jablońska, sounding much younger and more spry than she had imagined her to be. Apologies for not responding earlier, but there had been a crisis in the family, she had had to go to Łodz in a hurry, in fact she is still in Łodz. Apologies for not being able to open the apartment, apologies for missing

her visit, did she recover all the materials Witold left for her? Dear Witold, so sorely missed. And Ewa, always so busy, and now having to arrange everything from a distance: so inconvenient, such a pity!

She, Beatriz, is in no mood to listen to a torrent of words in an unfamiliar language (*un peu plus lentement, s'il vous plaît!*), but there are things she would like to know, things that only the Polish neighbour can tell her. Such as, for instance: what has been the fate of the apartment where she spent her solitary Polish night, an abode still haunted (if her experience counts) by the ghost of its master? Such as: aside from the poems, is she, Pani Jablońska, in possession of any supplementary message meant for her, Beatriz, the lady from Barcelona? Such as (if she can bring herself to ask): did the late lamented Witold ever show her his poems, in particular the first poem, with its metaphoric use of the word *rose*?

You must know, continues Pani Jablońska, that Witold owned not one but two apartments in the block—two adjacent apartments—and put in a communicating door—this was back in the 1990s, when everything was going cheap—but that unfortunately it was done without the proper paperwork, builders did things *à l'arabe* in those days, and now the apartment that is in fact two apartments with two postal addresses cannot be sold until the paperwork is regularized, which Ewa, poor Ewa, is having to do from Germany. Ewa got people to come with a truck and clear it out, the furniture, the books, everything, including Witold's piano, so at the moment it is standing empty, yet it can't be put on the market, such a tragedy.

À l'arabe: what can that mean? Or did she mishear?

'If I may interrupt,' she says, 'did Witold happen to say anything about me?'

There is a long, long silence. For the first time it occurs to her that the story of a sudden dash to Łodz may be fabricated, that Pani Jablońska may be not at all the wizened little old Polish widow dressed in black whom she has pictured to herself, that the very phrase *Witold's neighbour* may itself be a delicate euphemism not unconnected with the talk of a double apartment with a communicating door.

'If he didn't have anything to say, it doesn't matter,' she says, breaking the silence. 'Thank you for getting in touch. It is very kind of you.'

'Wait,' says Pani Jablońska. 'Is there nothing else you would like to know?'

'About Witold? No, Madame, I don't think so. I know all that I need to know.'

13. *Is there nothing else?* What was the woman threatening to tell? How poor Witold suffered? How he faced his death? No, she would prefer it if that were left in decent obscurity.

If she opens the gate a crack, who knows what might not come pouring through?

14. She calls Señora Weisz. 'I have decided that you should translate all the poems, from beginning to end. I will send the full set via courier to the travel agency, addressed to you, marked Personal. I don't want anyone else to see them. Can I rely on you?'

'You can rely on me. Poetry is not my strong point, but I will do my best. Perhaps you can make a down payment.'

'I will enclose a cheque with the file. Shall we say five hundred?'

'Five hundred would be good.'

15. After a week, a message from Señora Weisz. The translations are done. The bill comes to fifteen hundred Euros.

I will drop by and fetch the translations this evening, she replies.

The door is opened by a young man. 'Hi. You are the lady for the poems? Come in. I am Natán. My mother isn't home yet, but she won't be long. Please sit down. Do you want to see the poems?' He passes her a bulky packet: her photocopies plus the Spanish translations neatly printed out. She glances at the first one. *The lady between whose legs* is still there.

'I helped her now and again,' says Natán. 'Poetry isn't really my mother's thing.'

'You speak Polish too?'

'Not really. But I have read lots of Polish poetry. In Poland poetry is a disease, everyone catches it. Your poet—what is his name?'

'Walczykiewicz. Witold Walczykiewicz. He died not long ago. Have you been to Poland?'

'Poland is shit. Who would want to go there? It used to be bad. Now it's even worse.'

It dawns on her that they are Jews, Clara and her son, with good and sufficient reason not to like Poland.

'Walczykiewicz.' He pronounces the name like a native, better than she does, she between whose legs its bearer has lain. 'He is not a great poet, is he?'

'Poetry wasn't his medium. He was really a musician, a pianist. He was well known as an interpreter of Chopin.'

'The poems are pretty average, but there are a few that stand out. Are they about you?'

She is silent.

'He was in love with you, I would bet. If he knew you couldn't read Polish, why didn't he translate them for you?'

'Polish was his mother tongue. You can only write poetry in your mother tongue. At least that is what I was taught. Maybe it didn't matter to him that I couldn't read his poems. Maybe the important thing was to express himself.'

'Maybe. What I like best about them is that they aren't dry and ironic like everyone else's. Do you know Cyprian Norwid? No? You should read him. Walczykiewicz is like Cyprian Norwid, only not in the same class. His best poem—you will see it—is the one where he dives down to the seabed and finds himself face to face with a marble statue, and realizes it is Aphrodite—you know, the goddess. She has big painted eyes that look through him without seeing him. Eerie. I read somewhere that the Mediterranean is full of stuff from old shipwrecks—coins, statues, crockery, wine jars. I would like to go diving off the Greek coast sometime—who knows, I might be lucky.'

'Witold wasn't lucky.'

The boy looks at her oddly.

'I mean, he wasn't a lucky person. If he had gone diving he wouldn't have found a goddess. He would have come up empty-handed. Or he would have drowned. That's the way he was. What are you studying?'

'Economics. It isn't my thing, as my mother would say, but nowadays one has to. To get on.'

'I have two sons, a bit older than you. They didn't study economics but they have got on pretty well. They have made successes of their lives.'

'What did they study?'

'One studied biochemistry, the other studied engineering.'

There is more that she could say about her sons, much more, but she does not. She is proud of her sons, of the way in which they assumed responsibility for their lives early on, as though their lives were business enterprises that needed to be managed firmly and wisely. They take after their father, both of them. Neither takes after her.

'What are you going to do with the poems?' the boy asks. 'Will you be publishing them?'

'I don't think so. If they are not very good, as you say—and I am sure you are right—who would want to buy them? No, I won't publish them, but I did promise Witold before he died that I would take care of them, look after them. I can't find a better way to say it.'

Clara Weisz arrives, her arms full of packages. 'I'm sorry I'm late. Has Natán shown you the poems? I hope you like them. It wasn't as hard as I had feared, once we got going. An interesting man, Walczykiewicz. I looked him up on the Internet. As you say, he was a pianist, but did he tell you that when he was a young man, back in the 1960s, he published a book of verse? What we call a *publikacja ulotna*, a fleeting publication or fugitive publication. He wasn't popular with the authorities of the day.'

'I don't know much about his early life. He wasn't a very communicative man.'

'Well, it's all in the Polish Wikipedia, if you can read Polish.'

'Let me write you a cheque. You said fifteen hundred, less the advance?'

'That's correct. One thousand. I translated the handwritten notes too, but on separate pages. You will see.'

'Oh. I thought the handwritten bits were part of the poems—revisions, additions, that sort of thing.'

'No, I don't think so. But you can decide for yourself.'

She takes her leave. They will not see each other again, she and the Weiszes. A relief. They know too much about her. Yet what does it amount to, what they know? That she had an affair with a man? It happens every day. That the man was left heartbroken and wrote poems about her? That too happens, though not every day. No, the shame is that Clara Weisz, who is no one to her and no one to Witold, has had access to what was going on in Witold's soul, clearer access than she, for whom the poems were written, will ever have, given that there must be tones, echoes, nuances, subtleties in the Polish that no translation can ever transmit. Without the slightest effort Clara Weisz has become the Pole's first, best reader, with her son in second place, while she comes limping behind, a poor third.

16. She reads Clara's handiwork through from beginning

to end, rapidly. Not all the poems are comprehensible, though the prose versions are remarkably lucid. But by the end she has an answer to her overriding question. The poems are not an act of revenge, not at all. They are, in the broadest sense, a record of love.

She rereads a block of poems towards the end in which the phrases 'the other world' and 'the next life' come up repeatedly. The poems must date from when the Pole was facing death and trying to convince himself it was not the end of everything.

She tries to imagine what *deus ex machina* he could have thought would extract him from his present world, a world of loss and woe, and install him in the next one. As far as she can see, transport would be achieved in an instant, more or less magically. He would arrive in the next world a fully formed adult with an adult's bagful of memories and longings, to begin preparing for the day when she too will arrive, his Beatrice, to set up house with him in holy matrimony. She shivers. He cannot wait to see her again, but does she care to see him? The truth is that by the time the daughter phoned to announce his death she had all but forgotten him, or at least moved him into the no-longer-active bin.

Mourning is a natural process. All the peoples of the

planet have rituals of mourning. Even elephants. She, Beatriz, lost her mother early. The loss left a gaping hole in her life. She grieved, she mourned, she missed her. Then at a certain point the mourning came to an end and she moved on. But the Pole does not seem to have moved on. Having lost her, he mourned her and went on mourning, nursing his loss like a mother who refuses to give up a dead child.

He *says* he expects to be reunited with her in the next world, but what can that possibly mean? There must have been moments when, sitting alone in his dreary apartment in Warsaw, he knew he had seen the last of her. To make that real-life loss bearable he must have thrown all his failing powers into invoking, creating, calling into being a *new* Beatriz, a transfigured yet substantial version of herself, who, far from dismissing him and—even worse—forgetting him, was by secret, mystical means urging him to prepare a celestial home for her.

She does not believe in life after death, except in the most metaphorical of senses. When she is dead her children will remember her and reminisce about her, fondly or not so fondly. They might also pick her to pieces with their psychoanalysts (*Was she a good mother?*

Was she a bad mother?). As long as they go on doing so she will enjoy a flickering kind of life. But with the passing of their generation she will be tossed into a dusty archive, there to be shut out from the light of day for ever and ever. Such constitutes her belief, her mature, adult belief; and she does the Pole the credit of accepting that, when he was not absorbed in his music and his poetry, he shared it too—that he did not *really* believe there would be another life in another world where the two of them would find each other and enjoy the happiness that chance had withheld from them in their first incarnation.

So why write—and commit to her—these poems from his last months in which he looks forward so confidently to seeing her again, poems that steadfastly avoid the questions that dog any theory of the afterlife? Questions such as: Will the beloved not arrive attended by a host of spouses and lovers all looking forward to spending the afterlife by her side and in her bed? Will there be no jealousy in the afterlife? No boredom? No hunger? No bowel movements? What about clothes? Will we all have to wear shapeless smocks down to our ankles? And underwear—will a touch of lace be permitted or will everything have to be very plain, very puritan?

Heaven: a vast ante-room full of souls milling about in their uniform smocks, searching anxiously for their other halves.

17. It is not entirely true that he dodges the question of physical appearance. In one of his afterworld poems he writes that he and she will meet naked, and then confesses that in the present world—he must be referring to Mallorca—it was a matter of shame to him that he could bring to the table of love nothing but his ugly old male body.

18. Why is she so hard on him? Why does she hover over his poetic legacy with a scalpel at the ready? Answer: because she was hoping for more. It is hard to admit to, but she was hoping that the man who loved her would have used that love, that energy, that *eros*, to bring her to life better than he has managed to do. Vanity on her part? Yes, perhaps. But the Pole thought of himself as an artist in the grand old sense, a *maestro*, and an artist in the grand old sense (Dante!) would have given her a new life that was believable, that was proof against her own easy mockery. *For the lover the desired body is a soul.* The Pole loved her body. The Pole loves her soul (so he

says). But where in the poems does she see body transfigured into soul?

Señora Weisz's son thought the poems weak, and in most cases she agrees. Did the Pole see their weakness too? Did he see it, yet proceed nevertheless with his scribbling, keeping himself busy so that he would not have to see death sidling up to him?

With the whole of his pathetic project laid out before her on her desk, his project of resurrecting and perfecting a love that was never firmly founded, she is overcome with exasperation but also with pity. The picture grows clearer and clearer before her eyes: the old man at his typewriter in his ugly apartment, trying to force into life his dream of love, using an art that he was not master of.

I should never have encouraged him, she thinks. *I should have nipped the whole thing in the bud. But I did not see where it was leading. I did not see it was going to end up like this.*

She puts the translations back in their folder. Who else but she would ever want to read this stuff? All for nothing, all that patient labour, all that packing of one brick on top of another. There is not even a museum of bad poetry where it can be stored away, along with the rest of the lifeless verbiage that emerges from the hands of men like him, men who lack the art that quickens the word. *Poor old fellow!* she thinks. *Poor old guy!*

19. Did it occur to him that they might fail to meet in the afterlife not because there is no afterlife but because fate will have consigned him to the basement realm while she floats above in Paradise, eternally unattainable?

20. Or the reverse?

SIX

Dear Witold,

Thank you for the book of poems. You won't believe what a roundabout road they have taken, but at last they have arrived in a version I can read.

Natán, the son of my translator, a nice young man, though a bit forward, told me he liked the Aphrodite poem best, the one in which you sink to the bottom of the sea and meet Aphrodite in the form of a marble statue.

If Aphrodite is supposed to stand for me, if I am supposed to be Aphrodite, you have made a mistake. I am not that particular goddess. In fact I am not a goddess at all.

Ditto if I am supposed to be Beatrice.

You complain that the undersea Aphrodite looked straight through you without noticing you. For my part, I thought I saw you pretty well—saw you for what you were and accepted you. But perhaps you wanted more. Perhaps you wanted me to see a god in you, which I never did. My apologies.

A poem that touched me particularly was the one about yourself as a little boy receiving a lesson in anatomy from your mother. During all the time I knew you, I confess, I never once thought of you as a little boy. I treated you as a rational grown-up and expected you to treat me in the same way. That may have been another mistake. If we had dropped the adult masks and approached each other as child to child we might have done better. But of course, becoming a child is not as easy as it looks.

You made one or two proposals to me that I found disconcerting—for example that I run away with you to Brazil—but you never actually wooed me. Nor in the end did you seduce me. No seduction took place, as I think you will agree.

I would have liked to be wooed. I would have liked to be seduced. I would have liked to have been paid the sweet compliments and told the flattering lies that men tell the women they want to sleep with. Why? I don't know and don't care to know. A womanly longing, forgivable.

Why did you obey so meekly when I told you

to leave and go back to Valldemossa? Why did you not bombard me with pleas? *I cannot live without you!*—why did you never utter those words?

Theatrics, Witold—have you never heard of theatrics? Listen to Chopin. Listen to the Ballades. Forget about your own tight little readings. Open your ears, for a change, to the real Chopin performers, the enthusiasts who revel in the theatrics of his music and don't mind hitting a wrong key now and then.

And why did you not write to me, or call me, when you knew you were dying? It would have been so easy—so much easier than writing poems. Your neighbour says you did nothing in your last years but labour on your poems. She says you gave up music. Why? Did you lose faith?

If you were Dante, I would go down in history as your inspiration, your Muse. But you are not Dante. The evidence is before us. You are not a great poet. No one is going to want to read about your love for me, and—on mature consideration—I am glad about that, glad and relieved. I never asked to be written about, by you or by anyone else.

In case you have forgotten it, here is the poem I was referring to, in its new Spanish guise (no rhymes).

POEM 20
'Have *you* got one?' I asked my mother
as she dried me after my bath.
'No,' said my mother, 'I am the woman,
the one built to receive,
while you, my young man,
are the one built to give.
Your pipi is for giving—never forget that.'
'Give what, Mama?'
'Give joy. Give illumination. Give seed
so that again and again
season after season
the new crop will burst forth.'

Give seed—what did that mean?
I saw only darkly
As for *illumination*
I saw it not at all
not until she came to shine her light on my path
Beatrice.

Yet what did I give her
entering her body
the body of all women
the body of the goddess?
dead seed or no seed
no joy
no light

Courage, said Mama.
Like the serpent swallowing its tail
time has no end.
Always there is a new time
a new life
una vita nuova.
But now
my little prince
it is time for bed.

A nice poem, I am sure you will agree.
    Yours,
    Beatriz

Dear Witold,

A second letter. Don't worry, there won't be too many. I don't want to turn you into my secret friend, my phantom companion, my phantom limb.

To begin with, apologies for yesterday's rant. I don't know what got into me. You may not be Dante but your poems mean a great deal to me. Thank you for them.

I am writing to say I hope you didn't have too painful an end. When I visited the apartment in Warsaw I came across your ashes in a jar. Your daughter had forgotten to take them, or else they were delivered too late, after she had gone back to Berlin. The neglect of your remains strikes me as a bit casual, even by contemporary standards, if you don't mind my saying so. Surely there is a Heroes' Acre in Warsaw, or something like it, where you could be fittingly interred.

Both your daughter and your friend Madame Jablońska, who when I last heard was in Łodz visiting her family, have been discreet about the manner of your passing.

I raise the matter because of the handwritten words in the margin of the second-last poem, poem 83. I took the words to be part of the poem, but my translator disagrees. She points out that they don't fit anywhere, and furthermore are in neither Polish nor Italian but English. She calls them 'extra-poetic'. The words in question are: 'Save me, my Beatrice.'

If the words belong in the poem and 'Beatrice' is the heavenly being you have adopted from your friend and mentor Dante, well and good, I say no more. But if Beatrice is me, and if when you wrote those words you were pleading with me to save you—to come and save you from death—I must tell you, first, that the message did not reach me, telepathically or otherwise, and, second, that even if it had reached me I would probably not have come. I would not have come to you in Warsaw just as I would not run away with you to Brazil. I was fond of you (let me use that word), but not so extravagantly fond that I would have given up everything for you. You were in love with me—I have no doubt about that—and love is by nature extravagant. As for me, however, my feelings were more shaded, more complex.

That may seem a heartless thing to say at a time when you are defenceless, but it is not so intended. You had the whole creaking philosophical edifice of romantic love behind you, into which you slotted me as your *donna* and saviour. I had no such resources, apart from what I regard as a saving scepticism about schemes of thought that crush and annihilate living beings.

We can be honest with each other—can't we?—now that you are dead. What would be the point of pretending? Let us resolve to be honest yet never cruel.

In a spirit of honesty, I am not going to pretend that I like the very first poem in the series, and the coarse way in which you describe our physical relations. I suspect that your daughter got to see the poem, and that it coloured her attitude towards me. She treated me as if I were your whore.

Nor am I impressed by the second poem. I don't in general like men who stare at women. I don't find being stared at seductive—not in the slightest. And what is *chyme* (the translator's word)? The dictionary says it is a bodily fluid, but what is the sense of it?

POEM 2
Above all he craved to look on her,
he the old master, then a young buck.
Because he could not have her
(bared throat, flurry of skirts, unimaginable)
all the erotic charge ascended from his loins,
ascended through the blood, through the chyme,
to suffuse his living gaze.
Staring at her was his way of possessing her.
In public gatherings he would choose at random
some attractive girl
set her in his line of sight, seem to be sending her looks
(he called her his screen)
while secretly it was the farther one he was devouring,
his Beatrice
his quarry
la modesta, the modest one.
(Modesty high among her virtues:

modesty, grace, goodness.)
As for me, I had no luck,
came too late, lived too far away
had only her image to close my eyes on
poor fluttering little thing in the chambers of memory.

I find it a difficult poem—too difficult for me. I hope the translation does justice to it. You will be the best judge. The translator was not a professional.

La modesta. Thank you for that. Thank you for your high opinion of me. I will try to live up to it.

But it is getting late. Good night, my prince—time for bed. Sleep well. Sweet dreams.

Yours,

Beatriz

P.S. I will write again.

2022

AS A WOMAN GROWS OLDER

SHE is visiting her daughter in Nice, her first visit in years. Her son will fly out from the United States and spend a few days with them on the way to some conference or other. It interests her, this confluence of dates. She wonders whether there has not been some collusion, whether the two of them do not have some plan, some proposal to put to her of the kind that children put to a parent when they feel she can no longer look after herself. *So obstinate*, they will have said to each other: *so obstinate, so stubborn, so self-willed—how will we get past that obstinacy of hers except by working together?*

They love her, of course, otherwise they would not be cooking up plans for her. Nevertheless, she does feel like one of those Roman aristocrats waiting to be handed the fatal draught, waiting to be told in the most confiding, the most sympathetic of ways that for the general good one should drink it down without a fuss.

Her children are and always have been good,

dutiful, as children go. Whether as a mother she has been equally good and dutiful is another matter. But in this life we do not always get what we deserve. Her children will have to wait for another life, another incarnation, if they want the score to be evened.

Her daughter runs an art gallery in Nice. Her daughter is by now, for all practical purposes, French. Her son, with his American wife and American children, will soon, for all practical purposes, be American. So, having flown the nest, they have flown far. One might even think, did one not know better, that they have flown far to get away from her.

Whatever proposal it is they have to put to her, it is sure to be full of ambivalence: love and solicitude on the one hand, brisk heartlessness on the other, and a wish to see the end of her. Well, ambivalence should not disconcert her. She has made a living out of ambivalence. Where would the art of fiction be if there were no double meanings? What would life itself be if there were only heads or tails, with nothing in between?

'What I find unsettling, as I grow older,' she tells her son, 'is that I hear issuing from my lips words I once upon a time used to hear from old people and swore I would never say myself: *What is the world coming to!* for example. Thus: No one seems any longer to be aware that the verb *may* has a past tense—*what is the world coming to!* People stroll down the street eating pizza and talking into a telephone—*what is the world coming to!*'

It is his first day in Nice, her third: a clear, warm June day, the kind of day that brought idle, well-to-do people from England to this stretch of coast in the first place. And behold, here they are, the two of them, strolling down the Promenade des Anglais just as the English did a hundred years ago with their parasols and their boaters, deploring Mr Hardy's latest effort, deploring the Boers.

'Deplore,' she says: 'a word one does not hear much nowadays. No one with any sense deplores, not unless they want to become a figure of fun. An interdicted word, an interdicted activity. So what is one to do? Does one keep them all pent up, one's deplorations, until one is alone with other old folk and free to spill them out?'

'You can deplore to me as much as you like, Mother,' says John, her good and dutiful son. 'I will nod sympathetically and not make fun of you. What else would you like to deplore today besides pizza?'

'It is not pizza that I deplore, pizza is well and good in its place, it is walking and eating and talking all at the same time that I find so rude.'

'I agree, it is rude or at least unrefined. What else?'

'That's enough. What I deplore is in itself of no interest. What is of interest is that I vowed years ago I would never do it, and here I am doing it. Why have I succumbed? I deplore what the world is coming to. I deplore the course of history. From my heart I deplore it. Yet when I listen to myself, what do I hear? I hear my mother deploring the miniskirt, deploring the electric guitar. And I remember my exasperation. "Yes, Mother," I would say, and grind my teeth and pray for her to shut up. And so...'

'And so you think I am grinding my teeth and praying for you to shut up.'

'Yes.'

'I am not. It is perfectly acceptable to deplore what the world is coming to. I deplore it myself, in private.'

'But the detail, John, the detail! It is not just the grand sweep of history that I deplore, it is the detail—bad manners, bad grammar, loudness! It is the details that exasperate me, and it is the kind of detail that exasperates me, that drives me to despair. So unimportant! Do you understand? But of course you do not. You think I am making fun of myself when I am not making fun of myself. It is all serious! Do you understand that it could all be serious?'

'Of course I understand. You express yourself with great clarity.'

'But I do not! I do not! I express myself in words, and we are all sick of words by now. The only way left to prove you are serious is to do away with yourself. Fall on your sword. Blow your brains out. Yet as soon as I say those words you have to hide a smile. I know. Because I am not serious, not fully serious—I am too old to be serious. Kill yourself at twenty and it is a tragic loss. Kill yourself at forty and it is a sobering comment on the times. But kill yourself at seventy and people say, "What a shame, she must have had cancer."'

'But you have never cared what people say.'

'I have never cared what people say because I have always believed in the future. History will vindicate me—that is what I have told myself. But I am losing faith in history, as history has become today—losing faith in its power to come up with the truth.'

'And what has history become today, Mother? And, while we are about it, may I remark that you have once again manoeuvered me into the position of the straight man or straight boy, a position I do not particularly like.'

'I am sorry, I am sorry. It is from living alone. Most of the time I have to conduct these conversations in my head; it is such a relief to have persons I can play them out with.'

'Interlocutors. Not persons. Interlocutors.'

'Interlocutors I can play them out with.'

'Play them out on.'

'Interlocutors I can play them out on. I am sorry. I will stop. How is Norma?'

'Norma is well. She sends her love. The children are well. What has history become?'

'History has lost her voice. Clio, the Muse who once upon a time used to strike her lyre and sing of the doings of great men, has become infirm and frivolous, like the silliest sort of old woman. At least that is what I think some of the time. The rest of the time I think she has been taken prisoner by a gang of thugs who torture her and force her to say things she never meant to say. I can't tell you all the dark thoughts I have about history. It has become an obsession.'

'An obsession. Does that mean you are writing about it?'

'No, not writing. If I could write about history I

would be on my way to mastering it. No, all I can do is fume and deplore. And deplore myself too. I have become trapped in a cliché, and I no longer believe that history will be able to budge that cliché.'

'What cliché?'

'The cliché of the stuck record, which lost its meaning when gramophones and gramophone needles disappeared. The word that echoes back to me from all quarters is *bleak*. *Her message to the world is unremittingly bleak*. What does it mean, *bleak*? A word that belongs to a winter landscape yet has somehow become attached to me, like a little mongrel that trails behind, yapping, and won't be shaken off. I am dogged by it. It will follow me to the grave. It will stand at the lip of the grave, peering in and yapping *bleak, bleak, bleak!*'

'If you are not the bleak one, then who are you, Mother?'

'You know who I am, John.'

'Of course I know. Nevertheless, say it. Say the words.'

'I am the one who used to laugh but no longer laughs. I am the one who cries.'

Helen's gallery in the old city is, by all accounts,

successful. Helen herself does not own it. She is in the employ of two Swiss who descend from their lair in Bern twice a year to check the accounts and pocket the takings.

Helen, or Hélène, is younger than John but looks older. Even as a student she had a middle-aged air, with her pencil skirts and owlish glasses and chignon. A type that the French make space for and even respect: the severe, celibate intellectual. Whereas in England Helen would be cast at once as a librarian and a figure of fun.

In truth she has no grounds for thinking Helen celibate. Helen says nothing about her private life, but from John she hears of an affair that has been going on for years with a businessman from Lyon who takes her away for weekends. Who knows, perhaps she blossoms on her weekends away.

It is not seemly to speculate on the sex lives of one's children. Nevertheless, she cannot believe that someone who devotes her life to art, be it only the sale of paintings, can be without some secret fire.

What she had expected was a combined assault: Helen and John sitting her down and putting to her the scheme they had worked out for her salvation. But no, their first evening together passes perfectly pleasantly.

The subject is only broached the next day, in Helen's car, as the two of them drive north into the Basses-Alpes en route to a luncheon spot Helen has chosen, leaving John behind to work on his paper for the conference.

'How would you like to live here, Mother?' says Helen, out of the blue.

'You mean in the mountains?'

'No, in France. In Nice. There is an apartment in my building that falls vacant in October. You could buy it, or we could buy it together. On the ground floor.'

'You want us to live together, you and I? This is very sudden, my dear. Are you sure you mean it?'

'We would not be living together. You would be perfectly independent. But in an emergency you would have someone to call on.'

'Thank you, dear, but we have perfectly good people in Melbourne trained to deal with old folk and their little emergencies.'

'Please, Mother, let us not play games. You are seventy-two. You have heart problems. You are not always going to be able to look after yourself. If you—'

'Say no more, my dear. I am sure you find the euphemisms as distasteful as I do. I could break a hip, I could become senile; I could linger on, bedridden, for years:

that is the sort of thing we are talking about. Granted such possibilities, the question for me is: why should I impose on my daughter the burden of caring for me? And the question for you, I presume, is: will you be able to live with yourself if you do not at least once, in all sincerity, offer me care and protection? Do I put it fairly, our problem, our joint problem?'

'Yes. My proposal is sincere. It is also practicable. I have discussed it with John.'

'Then let us not spoil this beautiful day by wrangling. You have made your proposal, I have heard it and I promise to think about it. Let us leave it at that. It is very unlikely that I will accept, as you must by now have guessed. My thoughts are running in quite another direction. There is one thing the old are better at than the young, and that is dying. It behooves the old (what a quaint word!) to die well, to show those who follow what a good death can be. That is the direction of my thinking. I would like to concentrate on making a good death.'

'You could make just as good a death in Nice as in Melbourne.'

'But that is not true, Helen. Think it through and you will see it is not true. Ask me what I mean by a good death.'

'What do you mean by a good death, Mother?'

'A good death is one that takes place far away, where the mortal residue is disposed of by strangers, by people in the death business. A good death is one that you learn of by telegram: *I regret to inform you*, et cetera. What a pity telegrams have gone out of fashion.'

Helen gives an exasperated snort. They drive on in silence. Nice is far behind: down an empty road they swoop into a long valley. Though it is nominally summer the air is cold, as if the sun never touched these depths. She shivers, winds up the window. Like driving into an allegory!

'It is not right to die alone,' says Helen at last, 'with no one to hold your hand. It is anti-social. It is inhuman. It is unloving. Excuse the words, but I mean them. I am offering to hold your hand. To be with you.'

Of the two children, Helen has always been the more reserved, the one who kept her mother at more of a distance. Never before has Helen spoken like this. Perhaps the car makes it easier, allowing the driver not to look straight at the person she is addressing. She must remember that about cars.

'That's very kind of you, my dear,' she says. The voice that comes from her throat is unexpectedly low. 'I will not forget it. But would it not feel odd, coming back to France after all these years to die? What will I say to the man at the border when he asks the purpose of my visit, business or pleasure? Or, worse, when he asks how long I plan to stay? *Forever? To the end? Just a brief while?*'

'Say *réunion de famille*. He will understand that. A family reunion. It happens every day. He won't demand more.'

They eat at an *auberge* called Les Deux Ermites. There must be a story behind the name, but she would prefer not to be told it. If it is a good story it is probably made up anyway. A wind is blowing, cold as a knife; they sit behind the protection of glass, looking out on snowcapped peaks. It is early in the season: besides theirs, only two tables are occupied.

'Pretty? Yes, of course it is pretty. A pretty country, a beautiful country, that goes without saying. *La belle France*. But do not forget, Helen, how lucky I have been, what a privileged vocation I have followed. I have been able to move about as I wished most of my life. I have lived, when I have chosen, in the lap of beauty. The question I find myself asking now is, What good has it done me, all this beauty? Is beauty not just another consumable, like wine? One drinks it in, one drinks it down, it gives one a brief, pleasing, heady feeling, but what does it leave behind? The residue of wine is, excuse the word, piss; what is the residue of beauty? What is the good of it? Does beauty make us better people?'

'So that is the question: Does living with beauty make us good? Before you give me your answer, Mother, shall I give you mine? Because I think I know what you are going to say. You are going to say that all the beauty you have known has done you no good that you can see, that one of these days you are going to find yourself at heaven's gate with your hands empty and a big question mark over your head. It would be entirely in character for you, for Elizabeth Costello, to say so. And to believe so.

'The answer you will *not* give—because it would be out of character for Elizabeth Costello—is that what you have produced as a writer not only has a beauty of its own—a limited beauty, granted, it is not poetry, but beauty nevertheless, shapeliness, clarity, economy—but has also changed the lives of others, made them better human beings, or slightly better human beings. It is not just I who say so. Other people say so too, strangers. To me, to my face. Not because what you write contains lessons but because it *is* a lesson.'

'Like the waterskater, you mean.'

'I don't know who the waterskater is.'

'The waterskater or long-legged fly. An insect. The waterskater thinks it is just hunting for food, whereas in fact its movements trace on the surface of the pond, over and over, the most transcendentally beautiful of words, the name of God. The movements of the pen on the page trace the name of God, as you, watching from a remove, can see but I cannot.'

'Yes, if you like. But more than that. You teach people how to feel. By dint of grace. The grace of the pen as it follows the movements of thought.'

It sounds to her rather antique, this aesthetic theory her daughter is expounding, rather Aristotelian. Has Helen worked it out by herself or just read it somewhere? And how does it apply to the art of painting? If the rhythm of the pen is the rhythm of thought, what is the rhythm of the brush? And what of paintings made with a spray can? How would such paintings teach us to be better people?

She sighs. 'It is sweet of you to say so, Helen, sweet of you to reassure me. Not a life wasted after all. Of course I am not convinced. As you say, if I could be convinced I would not be myself. But that is no consolation. I am not in a happy mood, as you can see. In my present mood, the life I have followed looks misconceived from beginning to end, and not in a particularly interesting way either. If one truly wants to be a better person, it now seems to me, there must be less roundabout ways of getting there than by darkening thousands of pages with prose.'

'Ways such as?'

'Helen, this is not an interesting conversation. Gloomy states of mind do not yield interesting thoughts.'

'Must we not talk then?'

'Yes, let us not talk. Let us do something really old-fashioned instead. Let us sit here quietly and listen to the cuckoo.'

For there is indeed a cuckoo calling, from the copse behind the restaurant. If they open the window just a crack the sound comes quite clearly on the wind: a two-note motif, high-low, repeated time after time. *Redolent*, she thinks—Keatsian word—redolent of summertime and summer ease. A nasty bird, but what a singer, what a priest! *Cucu*, the name of God in cuckoo tongue. A world of symbols.

They are doing something they have not done together since the children were children. Sitting on the balcony of Helen's apartment in the suave warmth of the Mediterranean night, they are playing cards. They play three-handed bridge, they play the game they used to call Sevens, called in France *Rami*, according to Helen/Hélène.

The idea of an evening of cards is Helen's. It seemed an odd idea at first, artificial; but once they are into the swing of it she is pleased. How intuitive of Helen: she would not have suspected Helen of intuitiveness.

What strikes her now is how easily they slip into the card-playing personalities of thirty years ago, personalities she would have thought they had shed once they escaped from one another: Helen reckless and scatty, John a trifle dour, a trifle predictable, and she herself surprisingly competitive, considering that these are her own flesh and blood, considering that even the humble pelican will tear open its breast, if required to, in order to feed its young. If they were playing for stakes, she would be sweeping in her children's money by the veritable armful. What does this say about her? What does it say about all of them? Does it say that character is immutable, intractable; or does it merely say that families, happy families, are held together by a repertoire of games played from behind masks?

'It would seem that my powers have not waned,' she remarks after yet another win. 'Forgive me. How embarrassing.' Which is a lie, of course. She is not embarrassed, not at all. She is triumphant. 'Curious which powers one retains over the years and which begin to dwindle away.'

The power she retains, the power she is exercising at this moment, is one of visualization. Without the slightest mental effort she can see the cards in her children's hands, each single one. She can see into their hands; she can see into their hearts.

'Which powers do you feel you are losing, Mother?' asks her son cautiously.

'I am losing,' she says gaily, 'the power of desire.' In for a penny, in for a pound.

'I would not have said desire had power,' responds John, gamely picking up the baton. 'Intensity perhaps. Voltage. But not power, horsepower. Desire may make you want to climb a mountain but it won't take you to the top. Not in the real world.'

'What will take you to the top?'

'Energy. Fuel. What you have stored up in preparation.'

'Energy. Do you want to know my energetic, my

theory of energy? It is that, as we age, every part of our body deteriorates or suffers entropy, down to the very cells. Old cells, even when they are still healthy, are touched with the colours of autumn. This goes for the cells of the brain too: touched with the colours of autumn.

'Just as spring is the season that looks forward, so autumn is the season that looks back. The desires conceived by the autumnal brain are autumnal desires, nostalgic, layered in memory. They no longer have the heat of summer; even when they are intense, their intensity is complex, multivalent, turned more towards past than future.

'There, that is the core of it, my contribution to brain science. What do you think?'

'A contribution, I would say,' says her diplomatic son, 'less to science than to philosophy, to the speculative branch of philosophy. Why not just say that you feel in an autumnal mood and leave it at that?'

'Because if it were just a mood it would change, as moods do. The sun would come out, my mood would grow sunnier. But there are conditions of the soul that reach deeper than moods. *Nostalgie de la boue*, for instance: not a mood but a state of being. The question

I ask is, Does the *nostalgie* in *nostalgie de la boue* belong to the mind or the brain? My answer is, the brain. The brain whose origin lies not in the eternal realm of forms but in dirt, in mud, in the primal slime to which, as it runs down, it longs to return. A material longing emanating from the very cells themselves. A death drive deeper than thought.'

It sounds fine, it sounds like exactly what it is, chatter, it does not sound mad at all. But that is not what she is thinking, under all the chatter. What she is thinking is: *Who speaks like this to her children, children she may not see again?* What she is also thinking is: *Just the kind of thought that would come to a woman in the autumn of her years. Everything I see, everything I say, is touched with the backward look. What is left for me? I am the one who cries.*

'Is that what you are occupying yourself with nowadays—brain science?' says Helen. 'Is that what you are writing about?'

Strange question; intrusive. Helen never talks to her about her work. Not exactly a taboo subject between them, but out of bounds certainly.

'No,' she says. 'I still confine myself to fiction, you will be relieved to hear. I have not yet descended to hawking my opinions around. *The Opinions of Elizabeth Costello, Gentlewoman.*'

'A new novel?'

'Not a novel. Stories. Do you want to hear one of them?'

'Yes. It is a long while since you last told us a story.'

'Very well, for my children a bedtime story. Once upon a time, but in our times, not olden times, there was a man who travelled to a strange city, call it the city of X, for a job interview. From his hotel room, feeling restless, feeling in the mood for adventure, feeling who knows what, he telephoned for a call girl. A girl arrived and spent time with him. He was free with her, more free than he was with his wife; he made certain demands on her.

'The interview next day went well. He was offered the job and accepted, and in due course, in the story, moved to the city of X, wife and all. Among the people in his new office, working as a secretary or a clerk or a telephonist, he at once recognized the same girl, the girl who had come to his room. He recognized her and she recognized him.'

'And?'

'And I cannot tell you more.'

'But you promised us a story. What you have told us is not a story, just the premise for a story. Unless you go on, you have not kept your word.'

'She does not have to be a secretary. The man takes a job in the city of X and in due course is invited, with his wife, to the home of a colleague, and the colleague's daughter greets them at the door, and behold, it is the girl who came to his room in the hotel.'

'Go on. What happens next?'

'It depends. Perhaps nothing more happens. Perhaps it is the kind of story that comes to a halt and doesn't know where to go next.'

'Nonsense. It depends on what?'

Now John speaks. 'It depends on what passed between them in the hotel. Depends on the demands you say he made on her. In the story, Mother, do you spell out what demands he made?'

'Yes, I do.'

Now they are silent, all of them. What the man in the city of X will do next, or the girl with the sideline in prostitution, recedes into insignificance. The real story is out on the balcony, where two middle-aged children face a mother whose capacity to disturb and dismay them is not yet exhausted. *I am the one who cries.*

'Are you going to tell us what those demands were?' asks Helen grimly, since there is nothing else to ask.

It is late but not too late. They are not children, none of them. For good or ill they are all together now in the same leaky boat called life, adrift without saving illusions in a sea of indifferent darkness (what metaphors she comes up with tonight!). Can they learn to live together in their boat without devouring one another?

'Demands a man can make upon a woman that I would find shocking. But that you would perhaps not find shocking, coming from a different generation. Perhaps the world has sailed on in that respect and left me behind on the shore, deploring. Perhaps that is what turns out to be the nub of the story: that while the man, the senior man, blushes when he comes face to face with the girl, to the girl what happened in the hotel is just part of her trade, part of life, part of the way things are.'

The two children who are not children any more exchange glances. *Is that all?* they seem to be saying. *Not much of a story.*

'The girl in the story is very beautiful,' she says. 'A veritable flower. I can reveal that. The man in question, Mr Jones, has never involved himself in something like this before, the humiliating of beauty, the bringing down of it.

That was not his plan when he made the telephone call. He would not have guessed, when he made the telephone call, that he had it in him. It became his plan only when the girl herself appeared and he saw she was, as I say, a flower. It seemed an affront to him that all his life he should have missed it, real beauty, and would probably miss it from here onward too. *A universe without justice!* he would have cried inwardly, and proceeded from there in his bitter way. Not a nice man, on the whole, this Mr Jones.'

'I thought, Mother,' says Helen, 'that you had doubts about beauty, about its importance. A sideshow, you called it.'

'Did I?'

'More or less.'

John reaches out and lays a hand on his sister's arm. 'The man in the story, Mr Jones,' he says, 'he still believes in beauty. He is under its spell. That is why he hates it and fights against it.'

'Is that what you mean, Mother?' says Helen.

'I don't know what I mean. The story is not written yet. Usually I resist the temptation to talk about stories before they are fully out of the bottle. Now I know why.' Though the night is warm, she shivers lightly. 'I experience too much interference.'

'The bottle,' says Helen.

'Never mind.'

'This is not interference,' says Helen. 'From other people it might be interference. But we are with you. Surely you know that.'

With you? What nonsense. Children are against their parents, not with them. But this a special evening in a special week. Very likely they will not come together again, all three of them, not in this life. Perhaps, this once, they should rise above themselves. Perhaps her daughter's words come from the heart, the true heart, not the false one. *We are with you*. And her own impulse to embrace those words—perhaps it comes from the true heart too.

'Then tell me what to say next,' she says.

'Embrace her,' says Helen. 'In front of her family let him take the girl in his arms and embrace her. No matter how odd it looks. "Forgive me for what I put you through," let him say. Have him go down on his knees before her. "In you let me worship again the beauty of the world." Or words to that effect.'

'Very Irish Twilight,' she murmurs. 'Very Dostoevskian. I am not sure I have it in my repertoire.'

It is John's last day in Nice. Early next morning he will

set off to Dubrovnik for his conference, where they will be discussing, it seems, time before the beginning of time, time after the end of time.

'Once upon a time I was just a boy who liked peering through a telescope,' he says to her. 'Now I have to refashion myself as a philosopher. As a theologian even. Quite a life-change.'

'And what do you hope to see,' she says, 'when you look through your telescope into time before time?'

'I don't know,' he says. 'God perhaps, who has no dimensions. Hiding.'

'Well, I wish I could see him too. But I do not seem to be able to. Say hello to him from me. Say I will be along one of these days.'

'Mother!'

'I'm sorry. As I am sure you know, Helen has proposed that I buy an apartment here. An interesting idea, but I do not think I will take it up. She says you have a proposal of your own to make. Quite heady, all these proposals. Like being courted again. What is it that you are proposing?'

'That you come and stay with us in Baltimore. It is a big house, there is plenty of space, we are having another bathroom fitted. The children will love it.

It will be good for them to have their grandmother around.'

'They may love it while they are nine and six. They will not love it so much when they are fifteen and twelve and bring friends home and Grandma is shuffling around the kitchen in her slippers, mumbling to herself and clacking her dentures and perhaps not smelling too good. Thank you, John, but no.'

'You do not have to make a decision now. The offer stands. It will always stand.'

'John, I am in no position to preach, coming from an Australia that positively slavers to do its American master's bidding. Nevertheless, bear it in mind that you are inviting me to leave the country where I was born to take up residence in the belly of the Great Satan, and that I might have reservations about doing so.'

He stops, this son of hers, and she stops beside him on the promenade. He seems to be pondering her words, applying to them the amalgam of pudding and jelly in his cranium, passed on to him as a birth gift forty years ago, whose cells are not tired, not yet, are still vigorous enough to grapple with ideas both big and small, time before time, time after time, and what to do with an aging parent.

'Come anyway,' he says, 'despite your reservations. Agreed, these are not the best of times, but come anyway. In the spirit of paradox. And, if you will accept the smallest, the gentlest word of admonishment, be wary of grand pronouncements. America is not the Great Satan. Those men in the White House are just a blip in history. They will in due course make their exit, and all will be as it was before.'

'So I may deplore but I must not denounce?'

'Righteousness, Mother, that is what I am referring to, the tone and spirit of righteousness. I know it must be tempting, after a lifetime of weighing each word before writing it down, to just let go and be swept along in the torrent; but it leaves a bad taste in the mouth. You must be aware of that.'

'The spirit of righteousness. So that is what it sounds like. I will bear it in mind. As for paradox, the first lesson of paradox, in my experience, is not to rely on paradox. If you rely on paradox, paradox will let you down.'

She takes his arm; in silence they resume their promenade. But all is not well between them. She can feel his stiffness, his irritation. A sulky child, she remembers. It all comes flooding back, the hours it would take to coax him out of one of his sulks. A gloomy boy, son of gloomy parents. How could she dream of taking shelter with him and that tight-lipped, disapproving wife of his!

At least, she thinks, they do not treat me like a fool. At least my children do me that honour.

'Enough of quarreling,' she says (is she coaxing now? is she pleading?). 'Let us not make ourselves miserable talking about politics. Here we are on the shores of the Mediterranean, the cradle of Europe, on a balmy summer evening. Let me simply say, if you and Norma and the children can stand America no more, cannot stand the shame of it, the house in Melbourne is yours, as it has always been. You can come on a visit, you can come as refugees, you can come to *réunir la famille*, as Helen puts it. And now, what do you say we fetch Helen and stroll down to that little restaurant of hers on Boulevard Gambetta and have a nice meal together?'

2003–2007

THE OLD WOMAN
AND THE CATS

HE finds it hard to accept that, to have this ordinary if necessary conversation with his mother, he must come all the way to where she resides in this benighted village on the Castilian plateau, where one is cold all the time, where for supper one is given a dish of beans and spinach, and where in addition one has to be polite about these half-wild cats of hers that scatter in all directions every time one enters the room. Why, in the evening of her life, can she not settle down in some civilized place? It was complicated getting here, it will be complicated getting back; even being here with her is more complicated than it need be. Why must everything his mother touches turn complicated?

The cats are everywhere, so many of them that they seem to split and multiply before his eyes like amoeba. There is also the unexplained man in the kitchen downstairs, sitting silent and bowed over his own bowl of beans. What is this stranger doing in his mother's house?

He does not like beans, they are going to give him wind. To follow the diet of the nineteenth-century Spanish peasantry just because one is in Spain seems to him an affectation.

The cats, which have not yet been fed and will certainly not put up with beans, are all around his mother's feet, writhing and preening themselves as they try to attract her attention. If it were his house he would smite them all out. But of course it is not his house, he is only a guest, he must comport himself politely, even towards the cats.

'That's a cheeky little rascal,' he remarks, pointing—'that one there, with the white mark on its face.'

'Strictly speaking,' says his mother, 'cats don't have faces.'

Cats don't have faces. Has he made a fool of himself again?

'I mean the one with the white patch around its eye,' he corrects himself.

'Birds don't have faces,' says his mother. 'Fish don't have faces. Why should cats? The only creatures with proper faces are human beings. Our faces are what prove us human.'

Of course. Now he sees. He has made a lexical slip.

While human beings have feet, animals have paws; while human beings have noses, animals have snouts. But if only human beings have faces, then with what, through what, do animals face the world? *Anterior features?* Would a term like that satisfy his mother's passion for exactitude?

'A cat has a mien but not a face,' says his mother. 'A bodily mien. Even we, you and I, are not born with faces. A face has to be coaxed out of us, as a fire is coaxed out of coals. I coaxed a face out of you, out of your depths. I can remember how I bent over you and blew on you, day after day, till at last you, the being I called *you my child*, began to emerge. It was like calling forth a soul.'

She falls silent.

The kitten with the white blaze has become involved in a tussle with an older kitten over a strand of wool.

'With or without a face,' he says, 'I like that one's perkiness. Kittens promise so much. It's a pity they so rarely deliver.'

His mother frowns. 'What do you mean by *deliver*, John?'

'I mean that they seem to promise to grow into individuals, individual cats, each with an individual character and an individual outlook on the world.

But finally kittens just turn into cats, interchangeable, generic cats, representatives of their species. Centuries of associating with us don't seem to have helped them. They don't individuate. They don't develop proper characters. At most they exhibit character types: the lazy, the petulant, and so forth.'

'Animals don't have characters in just the same way that they don't have faces,' says his mother. 'You are disappointed because you expect too much.'

Though his mother is contradicting everything he says, he has no sense that she is hostile. She continues to be his mother, that is to say, the woman who bore him and then affectionately but abstractedly watched over him and protected him until he could find his own way in the world, and then forgot about him, more or less.

'But if cats are not individuals, Mother, if they are not capable of being individuals, if they are simply one embodiment after another of the Platonic Cat, why keep so many of them? Why not keep just one?'

His mother ignores the question. 'A cat has a soul but not a character,' she says. 'If you can grasp the distinction.'

'You had better explain,' he says. 'In simple terms, for the benefit of this slow-witted outsider.'

His mother turns on him a smile that is positively sweet. 'Animals don't have faces, properly speaking, because they do not have the fine musculature around the eyes and mouth that we human beings are blessed with in order that our souls may manifest themselves. So their souls remain invisible.'

'Invisible souls,' he muses. 'Invisible to whom, Mother? Invisible to us? Invisible to them? Invisible to God?'

'About God I don't know,' she says. 'If God is all-seeing, then all things must be visible to him. But invisible to you and me certainly. Invisible, strictly speaking, to other cats too: inaccessible to vision. Cats use other means to apprehend each other.'

Is this what he has travelled all these miles to hear: mystical nonsense about cat souls? And what of the man in the kitchen? When is his mother going to explain who he is? (This little house is not made for privacy, he can hear the man in the kitchen snuffling softly, like a pig, as he eats.)

'Apprehend each other,' he says: 'what does that actually mean—smelling each other's private parts, or something loftier? And'—he grows suddenly bolder—'who is the man downstairs? Does he work for you?'

'The man in the kitchen is named Pablo,' his mother says. 'I look after him. I protect him. Pablo was born in this village and has lived here all his life. He is shy, he doesn't respond well to strangers, that is why I didn't introduce you. Pablo went through a troubled period a while ago when he used to, as they say, expose himself. Expose himself habitually and without provocation. Not to me—after you have reached a certain age men no longer expose themselves to you—but to young women, and to children too.

'Social Services wanted to take Pablo away and lock him up in what they called a place of safety. His family, that is to say his mother and his unmarried sister, did not resist, he had caused them enough trouble. It was then that I stepped in. I promised the Social Services people I would look after him if they let him stay. I promised to keep an eye on him, to make sure he doesn't misbehave. Which is what I have done and go on doing. That is who is in the kitchen.'

'So that is the reason why you won't travel. Because you have to stay here to stand guard over the village exhibitionist.'

'I keep an eye on Pablo and I keep an eye on the cats. The cats too have an uneasy relation with the village. Generations ago these were ordinary domestic cats. Then people from villages like this began to drift away to the cities, selling their livestock, abandoning the household cats to fend for themselves. Of course the cats went feral. They went back to nature. What other choice did they have? But those people who have stayed behind in the villages don't like wild cats. They shoot them when they can, or else trap them and drown them.'

'Abandoned by their domesticators, they reoccupied their wild souls,' he offers.

The remark is intended flippantly, but his mother does not see the joke. 'The soul does not have qualities, wild or tame or anything else,' she says. 'If the soul had qualities it would not be a soul.'

'But you called it an invisible soul,' he objects. 'Isn't invisibility a quality?'

'There are no such things as invisible objects of perception,' she replies. 'Invisibility is not a quality of the object. It is a quality, a capacity or incapacity, of the observer. We call the soul invisible if we can't see it. That says something about us. It says nothing about the soul.'

He shakes his head. 'Where does it get you, Mother,'

he says, 'sitting by yourself in this godforsaken village in the mountains of a foreign country, splitting scholastic hairs about subjects and objects, while wild cats, full of fleas and God knows what other vermin, skulk under the furniture? Is this really the life you want?'

'I am preparing myself for the next move,' she replies. 'The last move.' She looks him in the eye; she is calm; she seems to be entirely serious. 'I am accustoming myself to living in the company of beings whose mode of being is unlike mine, more unlike mine than my human intellect will ever be able to grasp. Does that make sense to you?'

Does it make sense to him? Yes. No. He came here to talk about death, the prospect of death, his mother's death and how to plan for it, but not about her afterlife.

'No,' he says, 'it doesn't make sense to me, not really.' He dips a finger in the bean soup and stretches out his hand. The kitten with the white blaze pauses in its game, smells the finger cautiously, licks it. He looks the kitten in the eye, and for a moment the kitten looks back at him. Behind the eye, behind the black slit of the pupil, behind and beyond, what does he see? Is there a momentary flash, light glancing off the invisible soul hiding there? He cannot be sure. If there was indeed a flash, more likely than not it was his own reflection in the pupil.

Lightly the kitten leaps off the sofa, and, tail held high, strolls away.

'So?' says his mother. She is smiling faintly and perhaps even mockingly.

He shakes his head, wipes his finger clean on his napkin. 'No,' he says, 'I don't see.'

He sleeps in the little room fronting on the street. The room is so cold that he can barely bring himself to undress. He falls asleep curled in a ball under cold bedclothes. In the middle of the night he wakes, frozen. He reaches out to touch the little space heater that he had left switched on next to the bed. It is cold. He clicks the switch on the bedside lamp, but there is no light.

He gets out of bed, fumbles in the dark with the locks of his suitcase, puts on socks, trousers, a parka. He wraps a scarf around his head. Then with chattering teeth he gets back into bed and sleeps fitfully till dawn.

His mother finds him in the living room, huddled over the ashes of last night's fire.

'The electricity has cut out,' he says accusingly.

She nods. 'Did you switch on a heater in your room during the night?' she asks.

'I left the heater on because I was cold,' he says. 'I'm not used to this primitive way of life, Mother. I come from civilization, and in civilization we reject the notion that life has to be a vale of suffering.'

'Whether or not life is a vale of suffering,' says his mother, 'the fact is that in this house if you run a heater between 1 a.m. and 4 a.m., the hours when water is being heated for the bath, then the electricity will cut out.' She pauses, regards him levelly. 'Don't be childish, John,' she says. 'Don't disappoint me. We don't have many days left together, you and I. Let me see the best of you, not the worst.'

If his wife had said that kind of thing to him there would have been a fight—a fight, and a sour atmosphere that might have lasted for days. But from his mother he is, it seems, prepared to take a certain amount of chiding. His mother can criticize him and he will bow his head, within limits, even if the criticism is unjust (how was he supposed to know about the water heater?). Why, in his mother's presence, does he again become his nine-year-old self, as if the decades that have passed were nothing but a dream? Seated before the dead fire, he turns his face up towards her. *Read me*, he says to her, though he utters no word. *You are the one who claims that in the face the soul expresses itself, therefore read my soul and tell me what I need to know!*

'My poor dear,' says his mother, and reaches out a hand and ruffles his hair. 'We will need to toughen you up. If everyone were like you, we would never have made it through the Ice Age.'

'How many cats are you feeding?' he asks her.

'It depends on the time of year,' she replies. 'At present I feed a dozen regulars, plus some occasional visitors. In summer the numbers drop.'

'But surely, as you feed them, they multiply.'

'They multiply,' she agrees. 'That is the nature of healthy organisms.'

'They multiply geometrically,' he says.

'They multiply geometrically. On the other hand, nature takes its toll.'

'Nevertheless, I can see why your fellow villagers are perturbed. A stranger moves into their village and starts feeding the feral cats, and before long there is a plague of cats. Is there not a certain equilibrium that you are upsetting? And what of the horses that must end up as cat food so that you can feed these cats of yours? Do you spare a thought for the horses?'

'What do you want me to do, John?' says his mother. 'Do you want me to let the cats starve? Do you want me to feed only a select few? Do you want me to feed them tofu instead of animal flesh? What are you saying?'

'You could begin by having them neutered,' he replies. 'If you had them captured and neutered, one and all, at your own expense, then your neighbours in the village might actually thank you instead of cursing you under their breath. The last generation of cats, the neutered ones, could live out their lives contentedly, and that would be the end of it.'

'A win-win situation, in fact.' His mother sounds sharp.

'Yes, if you want to put it that way.'

'A win-win situation from which I emerge as a shining example of how the problem of feral cats can be addressed rationally and responsibly and yet with humanity.'

He is silent.

'I don't want to be an example, John.' In his mother's voice he hears the beginnings of the hard, insistent edge that he privately thinks of as obsessional. 'Let other people be examples. I follow where my soul leads me. I always have. If you don't understand that about me, you don't understand anything.'

'When the word *soul* is employed I generally cease to understand,' he says. 'I apologize for that. A consequence of my too rational education.'

He does not share his mother's obsession with animals. Faced with a choice between the interests of human beings and the interests of animals, he will opt without hesitation for human beings, for his own kind. Benign but distant: that is how he would describe his attitude to animals. Distant because, when all is said and done, there is a vast distance fixed between the human and the rest.

If it were up to him alone to solve the problem of this village and its plague of cats, if his mother were in no way involved—if his mother were deceased, for example—he would say *Kill them all*, he would say *Exterminate the brutes*. Feral cats, feral dogs: the world does not need any more of them. But since his mother is involved, he says nothing.

'Shall I tell you,' she says, 'the full story of the cats—of myself and the cats?'

'Tell me.'

'When I arrived in San Juan, one of the first things I noticed was that the local cats would slip away if they so much as caught a whiff in the air of a human presence. And with good reason: human beings had proved to be their pitiless enemies. I thought that a shame. I did not want to be anyone's enemy. But what could I do? So I did nothing.

'Then one day, while I was taking a walk, I spotted a cat in a culvert. It was a female, and she was in the act of giving birth. Because she could not flee, she glared at me and snarled instead. A poor, half-starved creature, bearing her children in a filthy, damp place, yet ready to give her life to defend them. *I too am a mother*, I wanted to say to her. But of course she would not have understood. Would not have wanted to understand.

'That was when I made my decision. It came in a flash. It did not require any calculation, any weighing up of pluses against minuses. I decided that in the matter of the cats I would turn my back on my own tribe—the tribe of the hunters—and side with the tribe of the hunted. No matter what the cost.'

She has more to say, but he interrupts her, he cannot let the opportunity pass. 'A good day for the village's cats but a bad day for their victims,' he observes. 'Cats are hunters too. They stalk their prey—birds, mice, rabbits—and, what is more, they eat them alive. How did you solve that moral problem?'

She ignores the question. 'I am not interested in problems, John,' she says—'neither in problems nor in solutions to problems. I abhor the mindset that sees life as a succession of problems presented to the intellect to be solved. A cat isn't a problem. That cat in the culvert made an appeal to me, and I responded. I responded without question, without referring to a moral calculus.'

'You met the mother cat face to face and you could not refuse her appeal.'

She regards him quizzically. 'Why do you say that?'

'Because it happens that yesterday you told me that cats do not have faces. And I remember how, when I was still a child, you used to lecture me on the gaze of the other, on the appeal that we dare not refuse when we meet the other face to face, unless we are to deny our own humanity. An appeal that is prior to and more primitive than the ethical—that was what you called it.

'The problem, you said, was that the very same people who talked about how we are interpellated by the other did not want to talk about being interpellated by animals. They would not accept that in the eyes of the suffering beast we may encounter an appeal that can likewise be denied only at heavy cost.

'But—I now ask myself—what exactly is it that, according to you, we deny when we refuse the appeal of the suffering beast? Do we deny our common animality? What ethical status does that curious abstraction have, *animality*? And what exactly is the appeal that comes to us from the animal's eyes, eyes that, according to you, lack the fine musculature necessary to express the soul? If the animal eye is simply an inexpressive optical instrument, then what you think you see in the animal eye may in fact be nothing but what you wish to see. Animals don't have proper eyes, animals don't have proper lips, animals don't have proper faces—I am happy to concede all of that. But if they don't have faces, how do we, we beings with faces, recognize ourselves in them?'

'I never said that the cat in the culvert had a face, John. I said that she saw in me an enemy and snarled at me. An ancestral enemy. A species enemy. What happened to me at that moment had nothing to do with an exchange of looks: it had to do with motherhood. I don't want to live in a world in which a man wearing boots will take advantage of the fact that you are in labour, unable to flee, vulnerable, helpless, to kick you to death. Nor do I want a world in which my children or any other mother's children will be torn away from her and drowned because someone has decided they are too many.

'There can never be too many children, John. In fact, let me make a confession, I wish I had had more children. This is nothing personal, but I made a lamentable mistake when I confined myself to just two the two of you, you and Helen—two children, a nice, neat, rational number that is supposed to prove to the world that the parents are not selfish, are not laying claim to more than their fair share of the future. Now that it is too late, I wish I had had lots of children. I would love to see children running in the streets again (have you noticed how dead a village like this one is without children?)—children and kittens and puppies and other small creatures, hosts of them, hosts and hosts.

'At the borders of being—this is how I imagine it— there are all these small souls, cat souls, mouse souls, bird souls, souls of unborn children, crowded together, pleading to be let in, pleading to be incarnated. And I want to let them in, all of them, even if it is only for a day or two, even if it is only so that they can have a quick look around this beautiful world of ours. Because who am I to deny them their chance of incarnation?'

'It's a pretty picture,' he says.

'Yes, it *is* a pretty picture. Go on. What more do you want to say?'

'It's a pretty picture but who is going to feed them all?'

'God will feed them.'

'There is no God, Mother. You know that.'

'No, there is no God. But at least, in the world I hope and pray for, every soul will have a chance. There will be no more unborn beings waiting outside the gate, crying to be let in. Each soul will have a turn to taste life, which is incomparably the sweetest sweetness there is. And at long last we will be able to hold up our heads, we masters of life and death, we masters of the universe. We will no longer have to stand barring the gate, saying, *Sorry, you cannot come in, you are not wanted, you are too many. Welcome*, we will instead be able to say, *come in, you are wanted, you are all wanted.*'

He is not used to his mother in this rhapsodic mood. So he waits, giving her every chance to return to earth, to qualify herself. But no, the mood does not leave her:

the smile on her lips, the glow of animation, the far-off gaze that does not seem to include him.

'Speaking for myself,' he says at last, 'I grant, it would have been nice to have more than just a single sister. The question that nags me, however, is this: If you had had to bring up a dozen children instead of two, where would Helen and I be today? How would you have afforded the expensive education that prepared us for the well-paid jobs and comfortable lives we are blessed with? Would I not, as a little boy, have been sent out to scavenge coals in the railyard or dig up potatoes in the fields? Would Helen not have had to go out and scrub floors? And what of yourself? With those many children clamouring for your attention, where would you have found the time to have lofty thoughts and write books and become famous? No, Mother: given a choice between being born into a small, prosperous family and being born into a big, poverty-stricken family, I would choose the small family every time.'

'What a peculiar way you have of looking at the world,' his mother muses. 'You remember Pablo, whom you met last night? Pablo had lots of brothers and sisters, but they went off to the big city, leaving him behind. When Pablo was in his hour of need, it was not his brothers and sisters who came to his rescue but the foreign woman, the old woman with the cats. Brothers and sisters don't necessarily love each other, my boy—I am not so naive as to believe that.

'You say that if you had to choose between being a professor at a university and being a farm labourer, you would choose to be a professor. But life does not consist of choices. That is where you keep going wrong. Pablo did not start out as some disincarnate soul facing the choice between being King of Spain and being the village idiot. He came to earth, and when he opened his human eyes and looked around, behold, he was in San Juan Obispo, and he was the lowest of the low. Life as a set of problems to be solved; life as a set of choices to be made: what a bizarre way of seeing things!'

It is hopeless to try to argue with his mother when she is in this mood, but he has one more stab. 'Nevertheless,' he says, 'nevertheless, you have chosen to intervene in the life of the village. You have chosen to protect Pablo from the social welfare system. You have chosen to play the saviour to the village's cats. You could have chosen quite differently. You could have sat in your study gazing out of the window, writing humorous sketches about life in rural Spain and sending them off to magazines.'

Impatiently his mother interrupts him. 'I know what a choice is, you don't have to tell me. I know what it feels like to choose to act. I know even better what it is to choose not to act. I could have chosen to write those silly sketches you speak of. I could have chosen not to involve myself with the village's cats. I know exactly how that process of deliberation and decision feels and tastes, exactly how little it weighs in the hand. The other way I speak of is not a matter of choice. It is an assent. It is a giving-over. It is a Yes without a No. Either you know what I mean or you don't. I am not going to explain myself further.' She rises. 'Good night.'

He goes to bed on this his second night in San Juan wearing a woollen cap, a sweater, pants, and socks, and sleeps the better for it. When he enters the kitchen in search of breakfast he is feeling almost genial; he is certainly hungry.

The kitchen is pleasantly bright and warm. From the old cast-iron stove comes a brisk crackling. Beside the stove, in a rocking-chair with a rug over his knees, sits Pablo, who is wearing glasses and appears to be reading the newspaper. '*Buenos días*,' he says to Pablo. '*Buenos días, señor*,' says Pablo back to him.

Of his mother there is no sign. He is surprised: she used to be an early riser. He makes himself coffee, helps himself to cereal and milk.

Now that he looks more closely, Pablo is not in fact reading but sorting through a heap of newspaper clippings. Most, carefully folded, go into a little fibre-board case that sits open on the floor beside him; a few he retains on his lap.

Given what his mother told him about Pablo, he expects the clippings to feature scantily clad women. But as if sensing his disapproval, Pablo holds up one to his gaze. '*El Papa*,' he says.

It is a photograph of John Paul II, robed in white, leaning forward in his throne, holding up two fingers in blessing.

'*Muy bien*,' he says to Pablo, and nods and smiles.

Pablo holds up a second picture. Again John Paul. Again he smiles. Is Pablo aware, he wonders, that the Polish pope is dead, that there is now a German on the throne? How long does news take to get to this village?

Pablo does not smile back, but he does open his lips and bare his teeth. His teeth are tiny, so tiny and so many as to remind him of a fish's; they seem to be coated in a white film, a film too thick and gummy to be saliva. This must be, he tells himself, what your teeth look like if you never brush them from one year's end to the next; and at once he is so revolted that he can eat no more. Holding his napkin to his mouth he rises. '*Scusi*,' he says, and leaves the room.

Scusi: wrong word, Italian. How do you say in Spanish that you are sorry, but you cannot bear to look your interlocutor in the face?

'Does he wash?' he asks his mother. 'I notice he doesn't brush his teeth. I don't know how you can bear to be near to him.'

His mother laughs gaily. 'Yes. And just imagine what sex would be like with him. But then, men are generally indifferent to the way they smell. Unlike women.'

They are sitting in the little back garden, the two of them, soaking in the rather pallid sun.

'And—do I understand correctly?' he says—'this man is to be heir to your Spanish estate? Is that a wise step? How can you be sure he will not shoo the cats away the moment you are gone?'

'How can I be sure of Pablo? How can we be sure of anyone? I could create a trust, I suppose, from which Pablo would receive a monthly stipend, and hire an agent to pay surprise visits to check that Pablo is doing his duty. But that would be too much like Kafka's castle—don't you think? No, the cats will have to take their chance with Pablo. If Pablo turns out to be a rotten egg, they will just have to go back to hunting to keep body and soul together. First the fabled years of plenty under Good Queen Elizabeth, then dark times under Bad King Pablo: if you are philosophical, as most animals are, you will shrug your shoulders and tell yourself that that's the way the world goes and get on with the business of living.'

'Still, Mother, to be serious for a moment, if you want to leave the village better off than you found it, might a legal trust not be a good option? Not a trust dedicated to keeping Pablo honest, but a trust that would take care of homeless animals? You could afford it.'

'*Take care of*…Be careful, John. In some circles *take care of* means *dispose of*, means *put down*, means *give a humane death*.'

'Take care without euphemism—that is what I mean. Offer them sanctuary and feed them and look after them when they are old or sick.'

'I'll consider it. Though I must say my preference is for something simpler. For giving Pablo my blessing and reminding him to feed the cats. Because it is for him too, this arrangement, unappetizing though you may find him. To show him he is trusted, who has never been trusted before. Maybe I will drop the Pope a line too, asking him to keep an eye on his servant Pablo. Maybe that will do the trick. Pablo is devoted to the Pope, as you must have noticed.'

It is Saturday, time for him to leave, to drive to Madrid and catch his flight back to America.

'Goodbye, Mother,' he says. 'I'm glad I had this chance to see you in your mountain hideout.'

'Goodbye, my boy. Give my love to the children and to Norma. I hope you have found this long trek worth your while. But ssh!'—she holds up a forefinger, not quite pressing it to his lips, that would not be her manner—'you need not tell me, you are only doing your duty, I know. There's nothing wrong with doing one's duty. It's duty that makes the world go round, not love. Love is nice, I know, a nice bonus. But not dependable, unfortunately. Doesn't always flow.

'But say goodbye to Pablo too. Pablo likes to feel included. Say to him *Vaya con Dios*. That's the old-fashioned way of putting it.'

He makes his way to the kitchen. Pablo is in his usual place, in the rocking-chair beside the stove. He reaches out a hand. '*Adios, Pablo,*' he says. '*Vaya con Dios.*'

Pablo rises to his feet, embraces him, gives him a kiss on each cheek. He can hear the little pop of saliva as Pablo parts his lips, smell the sweet foulness of his breath. '*Vaya con Dios, señor,*' says Pablo.

2008–2013

THE GLASS ABATTOIR

ONE

HE is woken in the early hours of the morning by the telephone. It is his mother. He is used by now to these late-night calls: she keeps eccentric hours and thinks the rest of the world keeps eccentric hours too.

'How much do you think it would cost, John, to build an abattoir? Not a big one, just a model, as a demonstration.'

'A demonstration of what?'

'A demonstration of what goes on in an abattoir. Slaughter. It occurred to me that people tolerate the slaughter of animals only because they get to see none of it. Get to see, get to hear, get to smell. It occurred to me that if there were an abattoir operating in the middle of the city, where everyone could see and smell and hear what goes on inside it, people might change their ways. A glass abattoir. An abattoir with glass walls. What do you think?'

'You are speaking of a real abattoir, with real animals being slaughtered, experiencing real death?'

'Real, all of it. As a demonstration.'

'I don't think there is the faintest chance that you

would get permission to build such a thing. Not the faintest. Aside from the fact that people don't want to be reminded of how the food comes to be on their plate, there is the question of blood. When you cut an animal's throat, blood gushes out. Blood is sticky and messy. It attracts flies. No local authority will tolerate rivers of blood in their city.'

'There won't be rivers of blood. It will just be a demonstration abattoir. A handful of killings per day. An ox, a pig, half a dozen chickens. They could make a deal with a restaurant nearby. Fresh-killed meat.'

'Drop the idea, Mother. You won't get anywhere with it.'

Three days later a package arrives in the mail. It contains a mass of papers: pages torn out of newspapers; photocopies; a journal in his mother's handwriting labelled 'Journal 1990–1995'; some stapled-together documents. There is a brief covering note: 'When you have time, glance over this stuff and tell me if you think something can be made of it.'

One of the documents is called 'The Glass Abattoir'. It starts with words attributed to someone named Keith Thomas. As early as the Middle Ages, says Thomas, municipal authorities in Europe began to regard the slaughter of animals in public as an offensive nuisance and took steps to remove the shambles to outside the town walls.

The words *offensive nuisance* are underlined in ink.

He skims through the document. It contains a more fully elaborated proposal for the abattoir his mother had described on the telephone, with a plan of its layout. Pinned to the plan are photographs of hangar-like buildings, presumably an existing abattoir. In the middle distance is a truck of the kind used for transporting livestock, empty and without a driver.

He calls his mother. It is four in the afternoon here, nine in the evening there, a civilized time for both of them. 'The papers you sent have arrived,' he says. 'Can you tell me what I am supposed to do with them?'

'I was in a panic when I sent them,' his mother says. 'It struck me that if I were to die tomorrow, the cleaning-woman from the village might sweep everything off my desk and burn it. So I packed the papers up and sent them to you. You can ignore them. The panic is over. It is perfectly normal to have accesses of dread as one grows older.'

'So there is nothing wrong, Mother, nothing I

ought to know about? Nothing but a passing access of dread?'

'Nothing.'

TWO

THE same evening he picks up the journal and leafs through it. It starts with several pages of prose headed 'Djibouti 1990'. He settles down to read.

'I am in Djibouti in north-east Africa,' he reads. 'On a visit to the market I watch a young man, very tall, like most people in this part of the world, naked above the waist, bearing in his arms a handsome young goat. The goat, which is pure white, sits peacefully there, gazing around, enjoying the ride.

'Behind the market stalls is an area where the earth and stones are stained dark red, almost black, with blood. Nothing grows there, not a weed, not a blade of grass. It is the slaughter-place, where goats and sheep and poultry are killed. It is to this slaughter-place that the man is bringing his goat.

'I do not follow them. I know what happens there: I have seen it already and have no wish to see it again. The young man will gesture to one of the slaughter-men, who will take the goat from him and hold the body to the ground, gripping the four legs tightly. The young man will take the knife from the scabbard that slaps against his thigh and without preamble slit the goat's throat, then watch while the body convulses and the life-blood pumps out.

'When the goat is finally still he will chop off his head, slit open his abdomen, pull out his inner organs into the tin basin that the slaughter-man will hold, run a wire through his hocks, hang him from the convenient pole, and peel off his skin. Then he will cut him in half, lengthwise, and bring the two halves, plus the head with its open but glazed eyes, to the market itself, where on a good day these physical remains will fetch nine hundred Djiboutian francs or five US dollars.

'Conveyed to the home of its buyer, the body will be cut into small pieces and roasted over coals, while the head will be boiled in a cauldron. What is not found to be edible, principally the bones, will be thrown to the dogs. And that will be the end. Of the goat as he was in the pride of his days no trace will remain. It will be as if he had never existed. No one will remember him save myself—a stranger who happened to see him, and happened to be seen by him, on his way to his death.

'That stranger, who has not forgotten him, now turns to his shade and asks two questions. First: *What were you thinking as you rode to market that morning in your master's arms? Did you really not know where he was taking you? Could you not smell the blood? Why did you not struggle to escape?*

'And the second question is: *What do you think was going on in that young man's mind as he carried you to market—you whom he had known since the day you were born, who were one of the flock he led out to forage every morning and brought home every evening? Did he breathe any word of apology for what he was about to do to you?*

'Why do I ask these questions? Because I want to understand what you and your brothers and sisters think of the deal that your forefathers struck with humankind many generations ago. In terms of that deal, humankind undertook to protect you against your natural enemies, the lion and the jackal. In return your forefathers undertook that, when the time came, they would yield up their bodies to their protectors to be devoured; furthermore, that their progeny unto the hundredth and the thousandth generation would do the same.

'It strikes me as a bad deal, weighted too heavily against your tribe. If I were a goat I would prefer to take my chance with the lions and the jackals. But I am not a goat and do not know how a goat's mind works.

Perhaps it is the way of the goat to think, *The fate that befell my parents and grandparents may not befall me*. Perhaps the way of the goat is to live in hope.

'Or perhaps a goat's mind does not work at all. We must take that possibility seriously, as certain philosophers do—human philosophers. The goat does not think, properly speaking, philosophers say. Whatever mentation occurs within the goat, if we had access to it, would be unrecognizable to us, alien, incomprehensible. Hope, expectation, foreboding—these are forms of mentation unknown to the goat. If the goat kicks and struggles at the very end, when the knife comes out, it is not because he has suddenly understood that his life is about to end. It is a simple reactive aversion to the overwhelming smell of blood, to the stranger who grips his feet and holds him down.

'Of course it is hard, if you are not a philosopher, to believe that a goat, a creature who seems so like us in so many ways, can go through life from beginning to end without thinking. One consequence is that, when it comes to the matter of abattoirs, we in the enlightened West do our best to preserve the ignorance of the goat or the sheep or the pig or the ox as long as is possible, trying to keep it from being alarmed until finally, as it sets foot on the killing floor and sees the blood-splashed stranger with the knife, alarm becomes unavoidable. Ideally we would want the beast to be stunned—its mind incapacitated—so that it will never ever grasp what is going on. So that it will not realize that the time has arrived for it to pay up, to fulfil its part of the immemorial deal. So that its last moments on earth shall not be filled with doubt and confusion and terror. So that it will die, as we put it, "without suffering".

'The males in the herds of animals we own are routinely castrated. Being castrated without anaesthetic is a great deal more painful than having your throat cut, and the pain endures far longer, yet no one creates a song and dance about castration. What is it, then, that we find unacceptable about the pain of death? More specifically, if we are prepared to inflict death on the other, why do we wish to save the other from pain? What is it that is unacceptable to us about inflicting the pain of dying, on top of death itself?

'In English there exists the word *squeamish*, which my Spanish dictionary translates as *aprensivo*. In English, *squeamish* forms a contrastive pair with *soft-hearted*. A person who does not like to see a beetle being squashed can be called either soft-hearted or squeamish depending on whether you admire that person's sympathy for the beetle or find it silly. When workers in abattoirs discuss animal-welfare people, people who are concerned that the animal's last moments on earth should be without pain or terror, they call them squeamish, not soft-hearted. They are generally contemptuous of such people. *Death is death*, say the abattoir workers.

'Would you like your own last moments on earth to be filled with pain and terror? the animal-rights people demand of the abattoir workers. *We are not animals*, reply the abattoir workers. *We are human beings. It is not the same for us as for them.'*

THREE

HE puts the journal aside and looks through the rest of the documents, most of which seem to be book reviews or essays on various writers. The shortest is entitled 'Heidegger'. He has never read Heidegger but has heard he is impenetrably difficult. What does his mother have to say about Heidegger?

'Concerning animals, Heidegger observes that their access to the world is limited or deprived: the German word he uses is *arm*, poor. Their access is not just poor in comparison with ours, it is absolutely poor. Though he makes this claim about animals in general, there is reason to believe that when he made this observation he had such creatures as ticks or fleas specifically in mind.

'By *poor* he seems to mean that the animal's world-experience has to be limited, by comparison with ours, because the animal cannot act autonomously, can only respond to stimuli. The tick's senses may be alive, but they are alive only to certain stimuli, for instance the odour in the air or the tremor in the ground that betrays the approach of a warm-blooded creature. To the rest of the world the tick may as well be deaf and blind. That is why, in Heidegger's language, the tick is *weltarm*, poor in world.

'What of me? I can think my way into a dog's being, or so I believe; but can I think my way into the being of a tick? Can I share the intensity of the tick's awareness, as its senses strain to smell or hear the approach of its desire? Do I want to follow Heidegger and measure the thrilling, single-minded intensity of the tick's awareness against my own dispersed human consciousness that flits continually from one object to another? Which is the better? Which would I prefer? Which would Heidegger himself prefer?

'Heidegger had a famous or notorious affair with Hannah Arendt while she was a student of his. In his letters to her, those that have survived, he says not a word about their intimacies. Nevertheless I ask: what was Heidegger seeking through Hannah, or through any other of his mistresses, if it was not that moment when consciousness concentrates itself in thrilling, single-minded intensity before being extinguished?

'I am trying to be fair to Heidegger. I am trying to learn from him. I am trying to get a grasp on his difficult German words, his difficult German thoughts.

'Heidegger says that to the animal (for instance the

tick) the world consists, on the one hand, of certain stimuli (smells, sounds), and on the other hand of all that which is not a stimulus and therefore may as well not exist. For this reason we can think of the animal (the tick) as enslaved—enslaved not to smells and sounds themselves but to an appetite for the blood whose proximity the smells and sounds signal.

'Total enslavement to appetite is patently not true of higher animals, which exhibit a curiosity about the world around them that extends well beyond the objects of their appetite. But I want to avoid talk of higher and lower. I want to understand this man Heidegger, towards whom I float the web of my own curiosity, like a spider.

'Because it is enslaved to its appetites, says Heidegger, the animal cannot act in and on the world, properly speaking: it can only *behave*, and furthermore can behave only within the world that is defined by the extent, the reach, of its senses. The animal cannot apprehend the other as and in itself; the other can never reveal itself to the animal as what it is.

'Why is it that, every time that I (like a spider) send out my mind trying to grasp Heidegger, I see him in bed with his hot-blooded student, the two of them naked under one of those capacious German eiderdowns on a rainy Thursday afternoon in Württemberg? Coitus is completed; they lie side by side, she listening while he talks, on and on, about the animal to whom the world is either a stimulus, a tremor in the earth or a whiff of sweat, or else nothing, blankness, inexistence. He talks, she listens, trying to understand him, full of goodwill towards her teacher-lover.

'Only to us, he says, does the world reveal itself as it is.

'She turns towards him and touches him, and suddenly he is full of blood again; he cannot have enough of her, his appetite for her is unquenchable.'

That is all. That is the abrupt end of his mother's three-page Heidegger piece. He hunts through the papers, but there is no fourth page.

On an impulse he telephones her. 'I have been reading your piece on Heidegger. I found it interesting, but what is it? Is it fiction? A piece of abandoned work? What am I supposed to make of it?'

'I suppose you can call it abandoned work,' his mother replies. 'It started seriously, then it changed. That is the trouble with most of the stuff I write nowadays. It starts as one thing and ends as another.'

'Mother,' he says, 'I am not a writer, as you know very well, nor am I an expert on Heidegger. If you sent me your story about Heidegger in the hope that I would tell you what to do with it, I am sorry to say I can't help.'

'But don't you think there is the germ of something there? The man who thinks the tick's experience of the world is impoverished, worse that impoverished, who thinks the tick has no awareness of the world beyond incessantly sniffing the air as it waits for a source of blood to arrive, yet who hungers, himself, for those moments of ecstasy when his awareness of the world shrinks to nothing and he loses himself in mindless sensual transports...? Do you not see the irony?'

'I do, Mother. I do see the irony. But is the point you are making not a trite one? Let me spell it out for you. Unlike insects, we human beings have a divided nature. We have animal appetites but we also have reason. We would like to live a life of reason—Heidegger would like to live a life of reason, Hannah Arendt would like to live a life of reason—but sometimes we cannot, because sometimes we are overtaken by our appetites. We are overtaken and we give in, we surrender. Then, when our appetites are satisfied, we return to the life of reason. What more is there to say than that?'

'It depends, my boy, it depends. Can we speak like grown-ups, you and I? Can we speak as if we both know what is meant by the life of the senses?'

'Go ahead.'

'Think about the moment in question, the moment when you are alone with the truly beloved, the truly desired. Think of the moment of consummation. Where is what you call reason at that moment? Is it utterly obliterated, and are we indistinguishable at that moment from the tick engorged with blood? Or, behind it all, does the spark of reason still glimmer, unextinguished, biding its time, waiting to flare up again, waiting for the moment when you separate yourself from the body of the beloved and resume your own life? If the latter, what has it done with itself, this spark of reason, while the body has been away, disporting itself? Has it been waiting impatiently to reassert itself; or has it on the contrary been filled with melancholy, wanting to expire, to die, but not knowing how? Because—speaking as one adult to another—is it not that which inhibits our consummations—that persistent little flickering of reason, of rationality? We want to dissolve into our animal nature but we cannot.'

'Therefore?'

'Therefore I think about this man Martin Heidegger who wants to be proud of being a man, *ein Mensch*, who tells us how he creates a world about him, *weltbildend*, how we can be like him, *weltbildend* too, but who actually is not sure, through and through, that he wants to be *ein Mensch*, who has moments when he wonders whether, in the larger perspective, it might not be better to be a dog or a flea and surrender yourself to the torrent of being.'

'The torrent of being. You have left me behind. What is that? Explain.'

'The torrent. The flood. Heidegger has intimations of what that experience would be like, the experience of the torrent of being, but he resists them. Instead he calls it an impoverished experience of being. He calls it impoverished because it is unvaried. What a joke! He sits at his desk and writes and writes. *Das Tier benimmt sich in einer Umgebung, aber nie in einer Welt*: the animal acts (or behaves) within an environment but never within a world. He lifts his pen. There is a knock at the door. It is the knock he has been listening for all the while he has been writing, his senses alert to it. Hannah! The beloved! He tosses the pen aside. She has come! His desire is here!'

'And?'

'That is all. I haven't been able to take it any further. All the stuff I sent you is like that. I can't take it to the next step. Something is lacking in me. I used to be able to take things to the next step, but I no longer seem to have it in me, that ability. The cogs are seizing up, the lights are going out. The mechanism that I used to rely on to take me to the next step no longer seems to work. Don't be alarmed. It is nature—nature's way of telling me it is time to come home.

'That's another experience Martin Heidegger wasn't prepared to reflect on: the experience of being dead, of not being present in the world. It's an experience all of its own. I could tell him about it if he were here—at least about its early manifestations.'

FOUR

A day later he leafs through his mother's journal again, settles on the last entry, dated July 1, 1995.

'Yesterday I went to a lecture by a man named Gary Steiner. He spoke about Descartes and the continuing influence of Descartes on our way of thinking about animals, even the more enlightened among us. (Descartes, one recalls, said that human beings have rational souls while animals do not. From which it followed that while animals are capable of feeling pain they are incapable of suffering. According to Descartes, pain is an unpleasant physical sensation which triggers an automatic response, a cry or a howl; whereas suffering is a different matter, on a higher plane, the plane of the human.)

'I found the lecture interesting. But then Professor Steiner started to go into detail about Descartes' anatomical experiments, and suddenly I could bear it no longer. He described an experiment that Descartes carried out on a live rabbit, which I presume was strapped down to a board or nailed to it so that it could not move. Descartes opened the rabbit's chest with a scalpel, snipping off the ribs one by one and removing them to expose the beating heart. Then he made a little incision in the heart itself, and for a second or two, before the heart stopped beating, was able to observe the system of valves by means of which the blood is pumped.

'I listened to Professor Steiner and then I stopped listening. My mind went elsewhere. I wanted urgently to fall to my knees; but we were in a lecture theatre with the seats very close to each other so that there was no space to kneel. "Excuse me, excuse me," I said to my neighbours, and worked my way out of the auditorium. In the foyer, which was empty, I was at last able to kneel and ask for pardon, on my own behalf, on Mr Steiner's behalf, on René Descartes' behalf, on behalf of all our murderous gang. There was a song hammering in my ears, an old prophecy:

> A dog starved at his master's gate
> Predicts the ruin of the state.
> A horse misused upon the road
> Calls to heaven for human blood.
> Each outcry from the hunted hare
> A fibre from the brain does tear…
> He who shall hurt the little wren
> Shall never be beloved by men…

> Kill not the moth nor butterfly
> For the Last Judgment draweth nigh.

'The Last Judgment! What mercy will Descartes' rabbit, martyred in the cause of science three hundred and seventy-eight years ago this year, and in God's hands since that day with his torn-open breast, show toward us? What mercy do we deserve?'

He, John, the son of the woman who fell on her knees in July of 1995 and asked for forgiveness, and then afterwards wrote the words he has just read, takes out his pen. At the foot of the page he writes: 'A fact about rabbits, attested by science. When the fox's jaws close on the rabbit's neck it, goes into a state of shock. Nature has so arranged it, or God, if you prefer to speak of God, has so arranged it, that the fox can tear open the rabbit's belly and feed on his innards and the rabbit will feel nothing, nothing at all. No pain, no suffering.' He underlines the words *A fact about rabbits*.

His mother has given no indication that she wants her journal back. But destiny is inscrutable. Maybe he will be the earlier of the two to die, struck down as he crosses the street. Then *she*, for a change, will have to read *his* thoughts.

FIVE

HE has come to the end of his reading. It is one in the morning here, six in the morning there. His mother is very likely still asleep. Nevertheless, he picks up the telephone.

He has a prepared speech. 'Thank you for sending the packet of documents, Mother. I have read through most of them, and I believe I see what you would like me to do. You would like me to hammer these miscellaneous pieces of writing into shape, make them fit together in some way. But you know as well as I do that I have no gift for that kind of thing. So tell me, what is this really all about? Is there something you are afraid to tell me? I know it is early in the morning, I apologize for that, but please be open with me. Is something wrong?'

There is a long silence. When at last his mother speaks, her voice is perfectly clear, perfectly lucid.

'Very well, I will tell you. I am not myself, John. Something is happening to me, to my mind. I forget things. I cannot concentrate. I have seen my doctor. He wants me to go in to the city for tests. I have made an appointment with a neurologist. But in the meantime I am trying to put my life in order, just in case.

'I can't begin to describe the mess on my desk. What I sent you is only a fraction of it. If something happens to me the cleaning-woman will throw it all in the trash. Which is perhaps what it deserves. But in my vain human way I persist in thinking that something of value can be made of it. Does that answer your question?'

'What do you think is wrong with you?'

'I don't know for sure. As I said, I forget things. I forget myself. I find myself in the street and I don't know why I am there or how I got there. Sometimes I even forget who I am. An eerie experience. I feel I am losing my mind. Which is only to be expected. The brain, being matter, deteriorates, and since the mind is not unconnected with the brain, the mind deteriorates too. That is how things are with me, in summary. I can't work, can't think in a larger way. If you decide you can't do anything with the papers, never mind, just put them somewhere safe.

'But while I have you, let me tell you what happened last night.

'There was a program on television about factory farming. Normally I don't watch such things, but this time for some reason I didn't switch off.

'The program featured an industrial hatchery for chickens—a place where they fertilize eggs en masse, hatch them artificially, and sex the chicks.

'The routine goes as follows. On the second day of their life, when they are capable of standing on their own two feet, the chicks are fed onto a conveyor belt, which moves them slowly past workers whose job it is to examine their sex organs. If you turn out to be female, you are transferred to a box for dispatch to the egg-laying plant, where you will spend your productive life as a layer. If you are male you stay on the conveyor belt. At the end of the conveyor belt you are tipped down a chute. At the bottom of the chute are a pair of toothed wheels that grind you into a paste, which is then chemically sterilized and turned into cattle-feed or fertilizer.

'The camera, last night, followed one particular little chick in his progress along the conveyor belt. *So this is life!* you could see him saying to himself. *Confusing, but not too challenging thus far.* A pair of hands lifted him, parted the fluff between his thighs, replaced him on the belt. *Lots of tests!* he said to himself. *I seem to have passed that one.* The belt rolled on. Bravely he rode it, confronting the future and all that the future contained.

'I can't put the image out of my mind, John. All those billions of chicks who are born into this beautiful world and are by our grace allowed to live for one day before being ground to a paste because they are the wrong sex, because they don't fit the business plan.

'For the most part, I don't know what I believe any longer. What beliefs I used to have seem to have been overtaken by the fog and confusion in my head. Nevertheless, I cling to one last belief: that the little chick who appeared to me on the screen last night appeared for a reason, he and the other negligible beings whose paths have crossed mine on the way to their respective deaths.

'It is for them that I write. Their lives were so brief, so easily forgotten. I am the sole being in the universe who still remembers them, if we leave God aside. After I am gone there will be only blankness. It will be as if they had never existed. That is why I wrote about them, and why I wanted you to read about them. To pass on the memory of them, to you. That is all.'

2016–2017

HOPE

THERE is a message on the answering machine, from his mother: 'Please telephone. It is about the final disposition.'

The final disposition: he is tired of the phrase. Not a month passes without the final disposition being raised—the final disposition of his mother's body, the final disposition of her worldly goods. He lives in Baltimore, MD. She lives in a village in Catalonia, six thousand kilometres away, in retreat from the world. What does he need to hear about the final disposition that he has not heard before?

He telephones. 'What news, Mother? How is your health?'

Her health is failing, it turns out: that is what this call is all about. 'I saw a specialist yesterday. I had to hire a car and driver to take me. The bus service has been cut, like everything else nowadays. The man says I have to prepare for the worst. He says I can no longer live alone.'

'Prepare for the worst. What is that a euphemism for—"the worst"?'

His mother ignores the question. 'I have instructed my agent that all communications henceforth should go to you. You will be the one making decisions, decisions about rights and royalties and so forth. After a while the decisions will begin to taper off, as I am forgotten. Then you will be free again.'

His mother is or was a writer. She stopped writing, as far as he knows, when she moved to the village five years ago. Already the world is in the process of forgetting her. Does she know that? The burden she is laying on his shoulders will not be heavy.

'What is it that you fear, Mother? What exactly did the specialist say?'

'He used the word *dementia*. I am showing signs of dementia. People around me see it. Sometimes even I see it. He says I cannot go on living alone. I need someone to be with me, to take care of me. At the very least.'

'At the very least?'

'He did not use the word *institution*, but it hung in the air between us. I might have to move, I might have to be moved, to an institution. I cannot face that, John. I am going to put an end to it. That is why I called.'

'Surely that is a long way off, a long way down the road—institutional care. And it won't be necessary anyway. You can come and live with us.'

'Thank you. I know you mean it. But it will not work. I am not going to inflict myself on you and Norma. A crazy old hag shuffling around the house. No, we need to settle the disposition of my things while I am still rational. Then I will be free to end it all.'

End it all. He does not know what to say. Because behind all this talk of final dispositions he hears something else, a plea: *Save me! Save me, my son!* A plea hidden in a cloud of obfuscation so that the fiction may be preserved that the two of them are rational beings discussing plans for the future.

His mother a rational being! What nonsense! Since before he was born his mother has been acting out one or other inner drama on the page. Every word she writes is the trace of something going on inside her. This very telephone call belongs to one of those dramas, the one called *The Death of Elizabeth Costello*.

'I am coming to see you, Mother. I can't come at once. I have duties at the university. But I will catch a flight on Friday. Will that be soon enough?'

He arrives in Barcelona at dawn after a sleepless

night on the plane. He hires a car, drives the two hours into the mountains to the village of San Juan, knocks at his mother's door. She opens the door herself. He is shocked by what he beholds. When he last saw her she was strong and erect, a woman of iron. Now he can only call her crumpled. Her cheeks have sunk in, her skin has a waxy colour; embracing her, he picks up odours of unwashed clothes, of old age.

'How are you, Mother?'

'On my last legs, as you can see. Have you had breakfast? Would you like some tea? The woman who does the cleaning will be here in a minute. Shall we sit down?'

He eases her into a chair. The house is a mess. Whoever does the cleaning does not take her job seriously.

'Tell me the story, the full story. You spoke of dementia but I see no sign of it.'

'Stay around and you will soon see the signs. I forget names. I forget words. I forget where I am. A while ago they found me out in the country, on a farm road, in my nightdress. I had no idea how I got there. I spent three days in hospital, undergoing tests, the full battery. Early dementia, they decided to call it: *dementia temprana*.'

'And there is no hope? No hope of a reversal? They say that playing an instrument is good for dementia. Or playing chess.'

'Of course there is hope. There is always hope. We live in hope. How else can we live? But hope is like grace. You can't bank on it. If you bank on it, it will not come. Like the angels. Like relying on an angel to stand over you, guarding you from evil. Out of the question. That is the law. That is how it works, this universe of ours. No angels. No interventions. Otherwise life would be too easy. So: yes, there is hope. But not for me. Kafka's words. One of his sayings. His paradoxes. He produced it as a joke, that was his manner, like a conjurer. A hat out of a rabbit. But it is true nonetheless, true for him and for you and for me. True for all of us. There is hope, only not for us. If salvation comes, it will come as a surprise. An overwhelming surprise.'

'Kafka. You remember his name. You remember his sayings. You make sense when you talk. This is not the behaviour of a demented person.'

'Early dementia. When the real thing comes I will forget everything, inexorably. All the names, then all the words, one by one. That is why I called. I need to show you where I keep things. After that I thought I would offer you a choice. Either you go back to your university in America, and your students and your duties, and I do the business myself; or you stay here in Catalonia while I do the business. I prefer the second. It is more practical, more efficient. You will not have to make a second trip. But it may be too much for you. I will understand.'

Do the business. He cannot believe what he is hearing. 'What do you mean, Mother, do the business?'

'You know what I mean, John. The words are crude, but that is because the business is crude. Do away with myself. Kill myself. Put an end to this life that has gone on too long. I have the means, the necessary. I have the pills. I am not afraid.'

She says she is not afraid, but he does not believe her. No one is not afraid.

'Would it help if I contacted your doctor, Mother? Does he speak English? I would like to know what exactly he meant by no hope. In my experience, doctors never say *no hope*. They always offer some ray of light, some cautious, professional ray of light.'

'No. This is not the kind of case in which there is a ray of hope.'

The front door opens: the woman who looks after

things. She peers into the living room, gives him a silent nod, then disappears into the kitchen.

'You offer me a choice, Mother, but it is not a real choice, and you know that. I can't leave you, knowing what you are going to do. I am going to stay with you. There is no question about that. But there is something I want you to acknowledge: that you called me here, that you want me by your side because you can't do it alone—*do the business*, as you call it. You want me to hold your hand. More than that. You want me to say, *Don't do it*. You want me to say, *There is always hope*.

'I want to tell you a story, Mother, a story about hope. We had a dog, a spaniel named Demeter. You never met her, but maybe the children talked to you about her—they were very fond of her.

'Late in life Demeter developed cancer, a huge tumour growing into the spinal column. We discovered it too late. There was nothing we could do except help her with the pain. So she lay in her basket in the kitchen waiting for death to come. But she had no thought of ending her life. If you put an ear to her throat you could hear a continual low growl of resistance, of defiance of her fate. She had no concept of hope yet she lived in hope. Hope became the medium of her being, the striving of each living cell of her body to go on living.

'That is the end of the story. Of course the dog died. We all die. But perhaps you can take a lesson from her.'

2019

THE DOG

THE sign on the gate says *Chien méchant*, and the dog is certainly *méchant*. Every time she passes by he hurls himself against the gate, howling with desire to get at her and tear her to pieces. He is a big dog, a serious dog, some sort of German shepherd or Rottweiler (she knows little about dog breeds). From his yellow eyes she feels hatred of the purest order shining upon her.

She ruminates on that hatred. She knows it is not personal: whoever approaches the gate, whoever walks or cycles past, will be at the receiving end of it. But how deeply is the hatred felt? Is it like an electric current, switched on when an object is sighted and switched off when the object has receded around a corner? Do spasms of hatred continue to shake the dog when he is alone again, or does the rage suddenly abate, and does he return to a state of tranquillity?

She cycles past the house twice every weekday, once on her way to the hospital where she works, once after her shift is over. Because her transits are so regular, the dog knows when to expect her: even before she comes into view he is at the gate, panting with eagerness. Because the house is on an incline, her progress in the mornings, going uphill, is slow; in the evenings, thankfully, she can race past.

She may know nothing about dog breeds, but she has a good idea of the satisfaction the dog gets from his encounters with her. It is the satisfaction of dominating her, the satisfaction of being feared.

The dog is a male, uncut as far as she can see. Whether he knows she is a female, whether in his eyes a human being must belong to one of two genders, corresponding to the two genders of dogs, and therefore whether he feels two kinds of satisfaction at once—the satisfaction of one beast dominating another beast, the satisfaction of a male dominating a female—she has no idea.

How does the dog know that, despite her mask of indifference, she fears him? The answer: because she gives off the smell of fear, because she cannot hide it. Every time the dog comes hurtling towards her, a chill runs down her back and a waft of odour leaves her skin, an odour that the dog picks up at once. It sends him into ecstasies of rage, this whiff of fear coming off the being on the other side of the gate.

She fears him and he knows it. Twice a day he can look forward to it: the passage of this being who is in fear of him, who cannot mask her fear, who gives off the smell of fear as a bitch gives off the smell of sex.

She has read Augustine. Augustine says that the clearest evidence that we are fallen creatures lies in the fact that we cannot control the movements of our own bodies. Specifically a man is unable to control the motions of his virile member. That member behaves as if possessed of a will of its own; perhaps even as if possessed by an alien will.

She thinks of Augustine as she reaches the foot of the hill on which the house sits, the house with the dog. Will she be able to control herself this time, will she have the willpower necessary to save herself from giving off the humiliating smell of fear? And each time she hears the growl deep in the dog's throat that might equally be a growl of rage or of lust, each time she feels the thud of his body against the gate, she receives her answer: not today.

The *chien méchant* is enclosed in a garden in which nothing grows but weeds. One day she gets off her bicycle, leans it against the wall of the house, knocks at the door, waits and waits, while a few metres from her the dog backs away and then hurls himself at the fence. It is eight in the morning, not a usual time for people to come knocking. Nonetheless, at last the door opens a crack. In the dim light she discerns a face, the face of an old woman with gaunt features and slack grey hair. 'Good morning,' she says in her not-bad French. 'May I speak to you for a moment?'

The door opens wider. She steps inside, into a sparsely furnished room where at this moment an old man in a red cardigan sits at table with a bowl of coffee before him. She greets him; he nods but does not rise.

'I am sorry to trouble you so early in the morning,' she says. 'I cycle past your home twice a day, and each time—no doubt you have heard it—your dog is waiting to greet me.'

There is silence.

'This has been going on for some months. I wonder whether the time has not come for a change. Would you be prepared to introduce me to your dog, so that he can familiarize himself with me, so that he can be shown I am not an enemy, that I mean no harm?'

The couple exchange glances. The air in the room is still, as if no window has been opened in years.

'It is a good dog,' says the woman. '*Un chien de garde,*' a guard dog.

By which she understands that there will be no introduction, no familiarization with the *chien de garde;* that because it suits this woman to treat her as an enemy she will continue to be an enemy.

'Each time I pass your house your dog goes into a state of fury,' she says. 'I have no doubt that he sees it as his duty to hate me, but I am shocked by his hatred of me, shocked and terrified. Passing by your home has become a humiliating experience. It is humiliating to be so terrified. To be unable to resist the fear, to put a stop to it.'

The couple stare at her stonily.

'This is a public way,' she says. 'I have a right, on a public way, not to be terrified, not to be humiliated. You have it in your power to correct this.'

'It is our road,' says the woman. 'We did not ask you to come here. You can take another road.'

The man speaks for the first time. 'Who are you? By what right do you knock at our door and tell us how to conduct ourselves?'

She is about to give her reply, but he is not interested. 'Go,' he says. 'Go, go, go!'

The cuff of the woollen cardigan he wears is unravelling; as he waves his hand to dismiss her it trails in his coffee. She thinks of pointing this out to him, but then does not. Without a word she retreats; the door is closed behind her.

The dog hurls himself at the fence. *One day*, says the dog, *this fence will give way. One day*, says the dog, *I will get to you and tear you to pieces*.

As calmly as she can, though she is trembling, though she can feel waves of fear pulsing from her body out into the air, she faces the dog and speaks, using human words. 'Curse you to hell!' she says. Then she mounts her bicycle and sets off up the hill.

2017

ACKNOWLEDGMENTS

My thanks to Maria Soledad Costantini, Mariana Dimópulos, Georges Lory, Valerie Miles and Dolores Udina for counsel and advice during the composition of 'The Pole'.

'The Pole' was published, in Spanish translation, as *El Polaco*, El Hilo de Ariadna, Buenos Aires, 2022.

The quotation in 'The Glass Abattoir' from 'Auguries of Innocence' comes from William Blake's *Poetical Works*, ed. John Sampson, OUP, 1913.

An earlier version of 'As a Woman Grows Older' was published in *The New York Review of Books*, 15 January 2004.

Earlier versions of 'The Old Woman and the Cats' were published, in Italian translation, in *Aut Aut*, September 2014; and, in Spanish translation, in *Siete cuentos morales*, El Hilo de Ariadna, Buenos Aires, 2018.

'The Glass Abattoir' was published in the *Monthly*, December 2022. An earlier version was published, in Spanish translation, in *Siete cuentos morales*, 2018.

An earlier version of 'Hope' was published, in Italian translation, in *La Repubblica*, 26 June 2019.

'The Dog' appeared in *The New Yorker*, 4 December 2017.

penguin.co.uk/vintage

EXPL💥DAPEDIA

Welcome to *Explodapedia*, the indispensable guide to everything you need to know!

This series is packed with in-depth knowledge you can trust; it gives you the tools you need to understand the science behind the wonders of our world. Read on to learn how nature can heal our wounded planet in *Rewild* . . .

'I am in love with this book! It's joyful, fascinating, galvanising, beautifully written, accessible . . . it's an eye-opener and I can't wait to share it with all the children I know, and their parents.'
Isabella Tree, author & conservationist

'Imbued with hope, humour and joy. This is a book that needs to be read by every school kid, everywhere, and their parents.'
Lee Schofield, author & ecologist

'*Rewild* is truly magical . . . Young or old, people are going to love this book.' **Ben Goldsmith, author & environmentalist**

'A must-read for all young people who are interested in the concept of rewilding and nature recovery.' **Derek Gow, author**

'*Rewild* gives you a real sense of how connected and rich the diversity of life is, as well as how it's in peril . . . This book will inspire and inform the next generation.'
Leif Bersweden, writer, botanist, science communicator

*BM: To Beda. Thank you for rewilding our lives.
May your generation – and those to come – find ways
to thrive amid a wilder future. x*

MA: For Connor and Spencer, finally released into the wild.